GOSCINNY AND UDERZO
PRESENT
An Asterix Adventure

ASTERIX
AND THE
FALLING SKY

Written and Illustrated by ALBERT UDERZO

Translated by Anthea Bell *and* Derek Hockridge

For my brother Bruno, to whom I owe everything.

Bruno (1920-2004) and Albert Uderzo in 1942

Bruno Uderzo was Albert's elder brother. There were seven years between them. It was Bruno who, recognising his younger brother's budding talent, first took him to see a Parisian publisher. That was in the summer of 1940, and Albert was thirteen years old.

Respect, affection and shared interests united the two brothers.

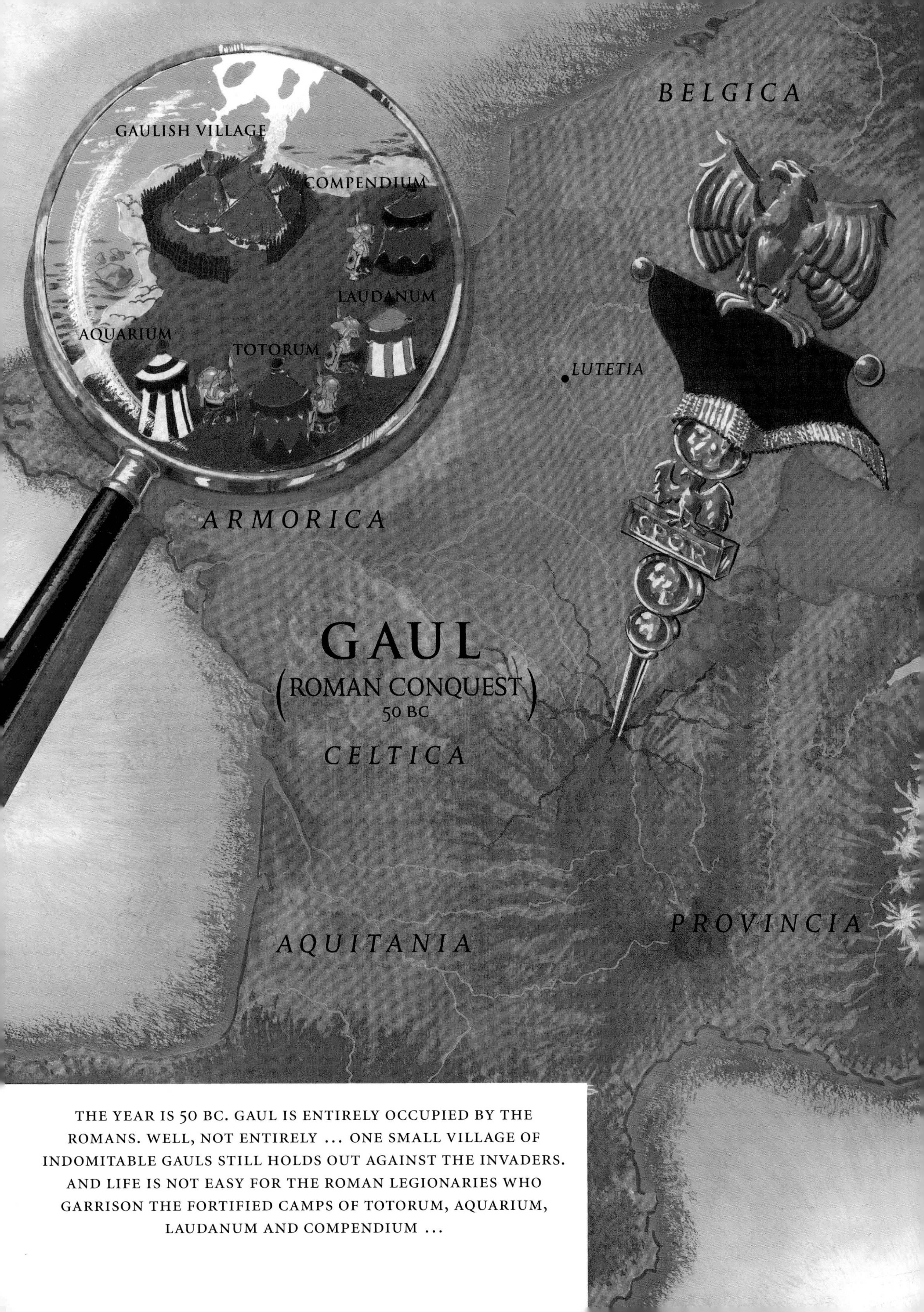
GAULISH VILLAGE
COMPENDIUM
LAUDANUM
AQUARIUM
TOTORUM
BELGICA
LUTETIA
SPQR
ARMORICA
GAUL
(ROMAN CONQUEST)
50 BC
CELTICA
AQUITANIA
PROVINCIA

THE YEAR IS 50 BC. GAUL IS ENTIRELY OCCUPIED BY THE ROMANS. WELL, NOT ENTIRELY ... ONE SMALL VILLAGE OF INDOMITABLE GAULS STILL HOLDS OUT AGAINST THE INVADERS. AND LIFE IS NOT EASY FOR THE ROMAN LEGIONARIES WHO GARRISON THE FORTIFIED CAMPS OF TOTORUM, AQUARIUM, LAUDANUM AND COMPENDIUM ...

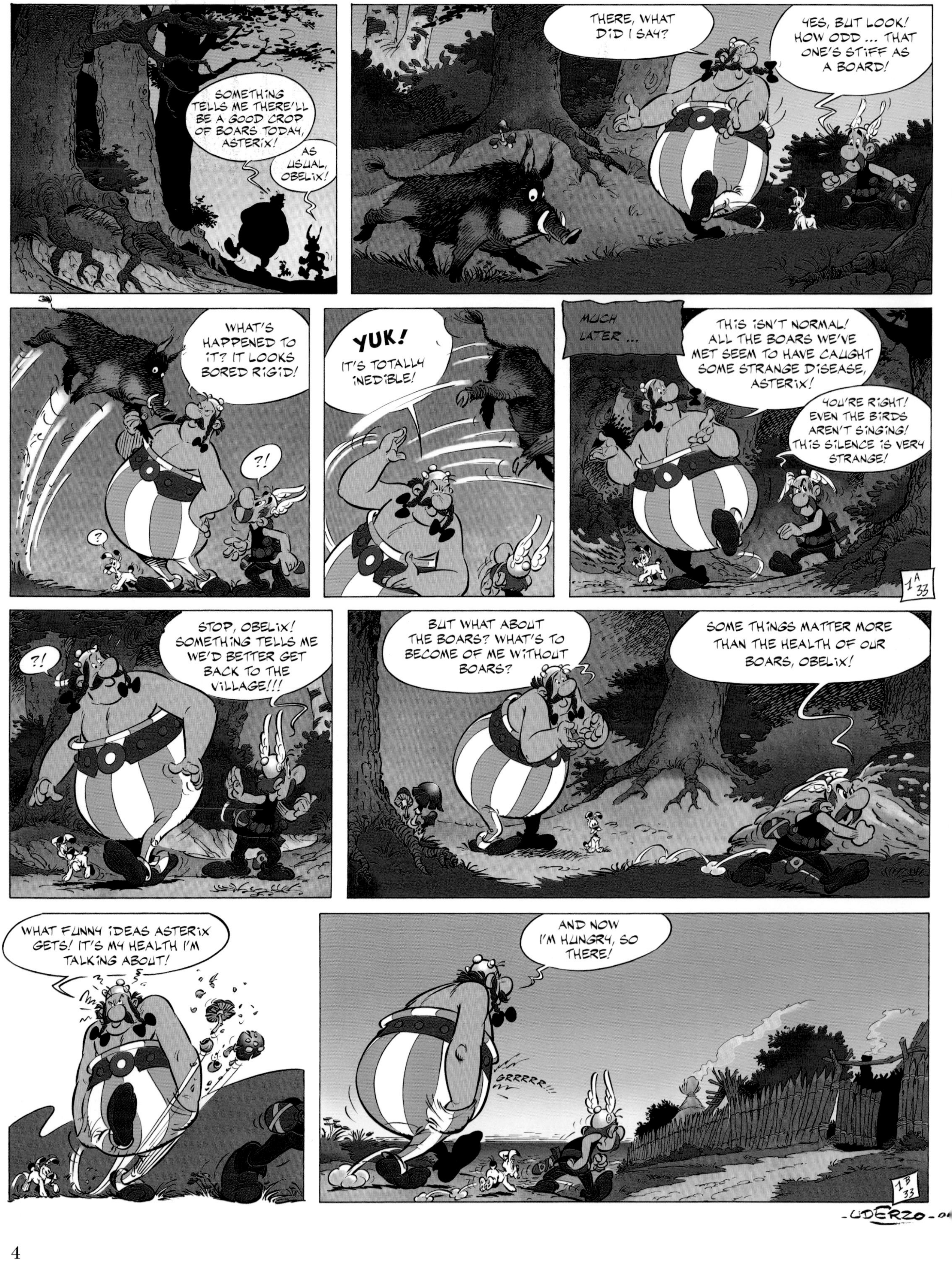
SOMETHING TELLS ME THERE'LL BE A GOOD CROP OF BOARS TODAY, ASTERIX!
AS USUAL, OBELIX!
THERE, WHAT DID I SAY?
YES, BUT LOOK! HOW ODD ... THAT ONE'S STIFF AS A BOARD!
WHAT'S HAPPENED TO IT? IT LOOKS BORED RIGID!
?!
?
YUK!
IT'S TOTALLY INEDIBLE!
MUCH LATER ...
THIS ISN'T NORMAL! ALL THE BOARS WE'VE MET SEEM TO HAVE CAUGHT SOME STRANGE DISEASE, ASTERIX!
YOU'RE RIGHT! EVEN THE BIRDS AREN'T SINGING! THIS SILENCE IS VERY STRANGE!
?!
STOP, OBELIX! SOMETHING TELLS ME WE'D BETTER GET BACK TO THE VILLAGE!!!
BUT WHAT ABOUT THE BOARS? WHAT'S TO BECOME OF ME WITHOUT BOARS?
SOME THINGS MATTER MORE THAN THE HEALTH OF OUR BOARS, OBELIX!
WHAT FUNNY IDEAS ASTERIX GETS! IT'S MY HEALTH I'M TALKING ABOUT!
AND NOW I'M HUNGRY, SO THERE!
GRRRRR!!!
UDERZO

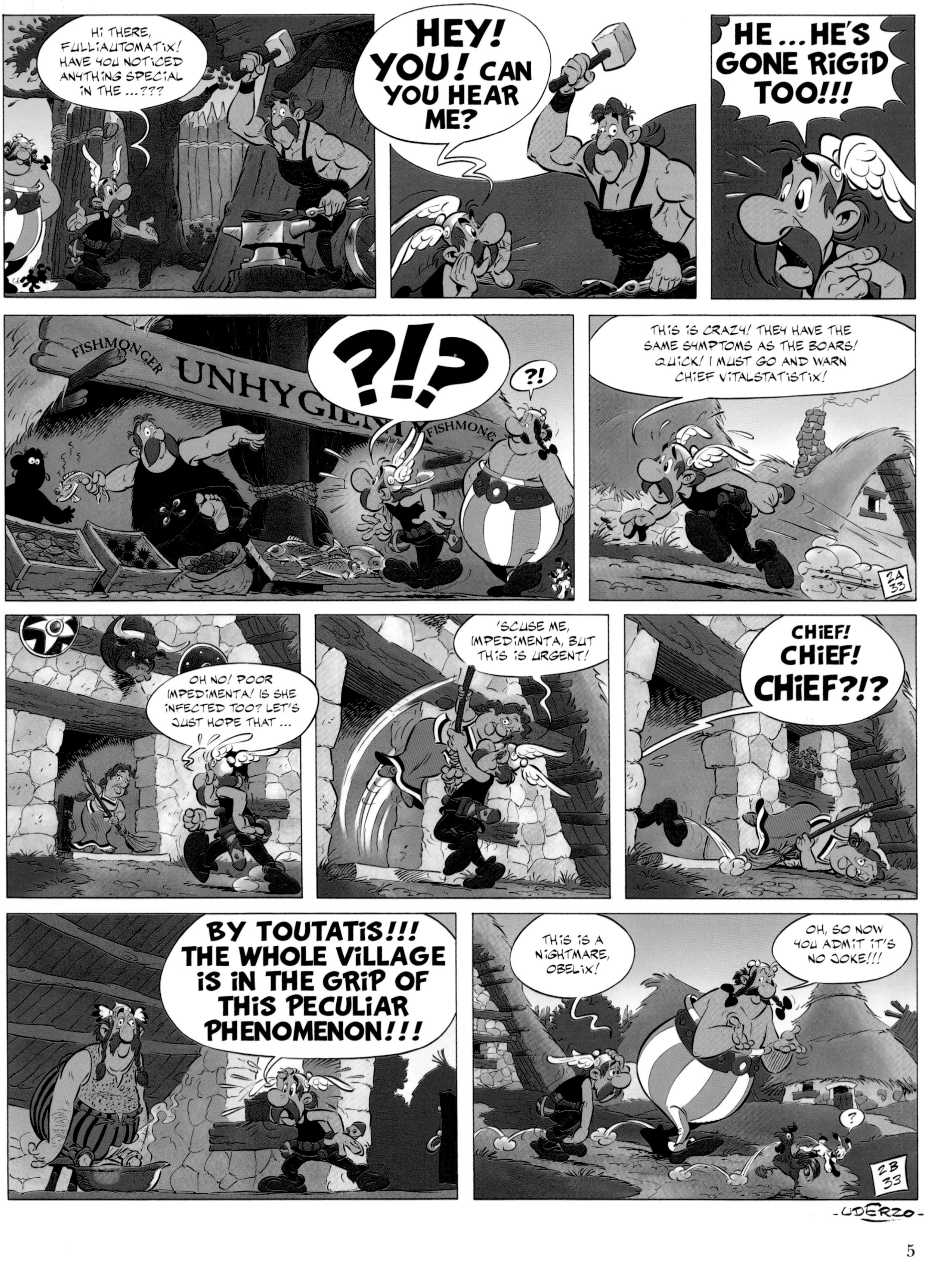
HI THERE, FULLIAUTOMATIX! HAVE YOU NOTICED ANYTHING SPECIAL IN THE ...???
HEY! YOU! CAN YOU HEAR ME?
HE ... HE'S GONE RIGID TOO!!!
FISHMONGER
UNHYGIENIX
FISHMONG
?!?
?!
THIS IS CRAZY! THEY HAVE THE SAME SYMPTOMS AS THE BOARS! QUICK! I MUST GO AND WARN CHIEF VITALSTATISTIX!
2A 33
OH NO! POOR IMPEDIMENTA! IS SHE INFECTED TOO? LET'S JUST HOPE THAT ...
'SCUSE ME, IMPEDIMENTA, BUT THIS IS URGENT!
CHIEF! CHIEF! CHIEF?!?
BY TOUTATIS!!! THE WHOLE VILLAGE IS IN THE GRIP OF THIS PECULIAR PHENOMENON!!!
THIS IS A NIGHTMARE, OBELIX!
OH, SO NOW YOU ADMIT IT'S NO JOKE!!!
?
2B 33
-UDERZO-

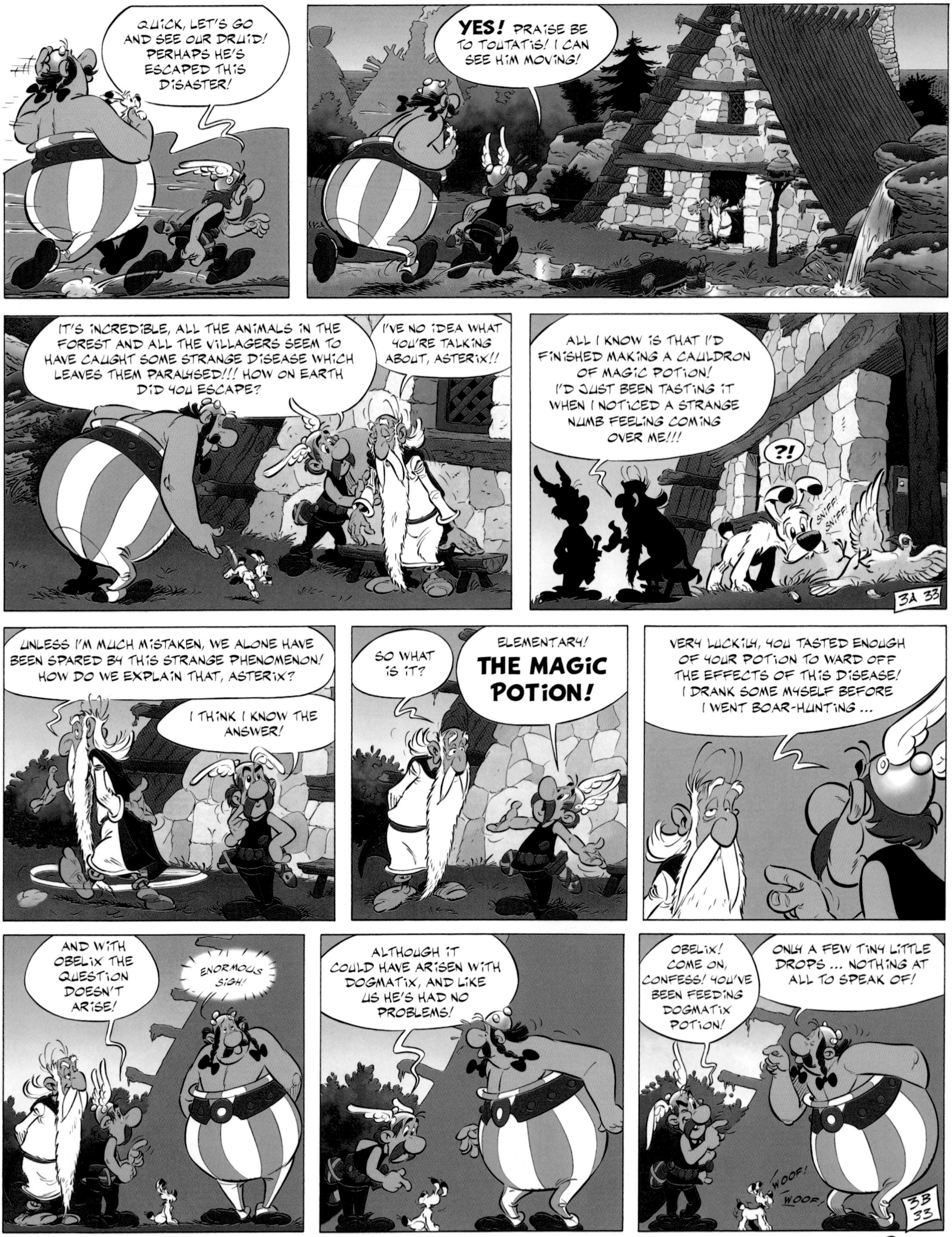
QUICK, LET'S GO AND SEE OUR DRUID! PERHAPS HE'S ESCAPED THIS DISASTER!
YES! PRAISE BE TO TOUTATIS! I CAN SEE HIM MOVING!
IT'S INCREDIBLE, ALL THE ANIMALS IN THE FOREST AND ALL THE VILLAGERS SEEM TO HAVE CAUGHT SOME STRANGE DISEASE WHICH LEAVES THEM PARALYSED!!! HOW ON EARTH DID YOU ESCAPE?
I'VE NO IDEA WHAT YOU'RE TALKING ABOUT, ASTERIX!!
ALL I KNOW IS THAT I'D FINISHED MAKING A CAULDRON OF MAGIC POTION! I'D JUST BEEN TASTING IT WHEN I NOTICED A STRANGE NUMB FEELING COMING OVER ME!!!
?!
SNIFF! SNIFF!
3A 33
UNLESS I'M MUCH MISTAKEN, WE ALONE HAVE BEEN SPARED BY THIS STRANGE PHENOMENON! HOW DO WE EXPLAIN THAT, ASTERIX?
I THINK I KNOW THE ANSWER!
SO WHAT IS IT?
ELEMENTARY! THE MAGIC POTION!
VERY LUCKILY, YOU TASTED ENOUGH OF YOUR POTION TO WARD OFF THE EFFECTS OF THIS DISEASE! I DRANK SOME MYSELF BEFORE I WENT BOAR-HUNTING ...
AND WITH OBELIX THE QUESTION DOESN'T ARISE!
ENORMOUS SIGH!
ALTHOUGH IT COULD HAVE ARISEN WITH DOGMATIX, AND LIKE US HE'S HAD NO PROBLEMS!
OBELIX! COME ON, CONFESS! YOU'VE BEEN FEEDING DOGMATIX POTION!
ONLY A FEW TINY LITTLE DROPS ... NOTHING AT ALL TO SPEAK OF!
WOOF! WOOF!
3B 33
- UDERZO -

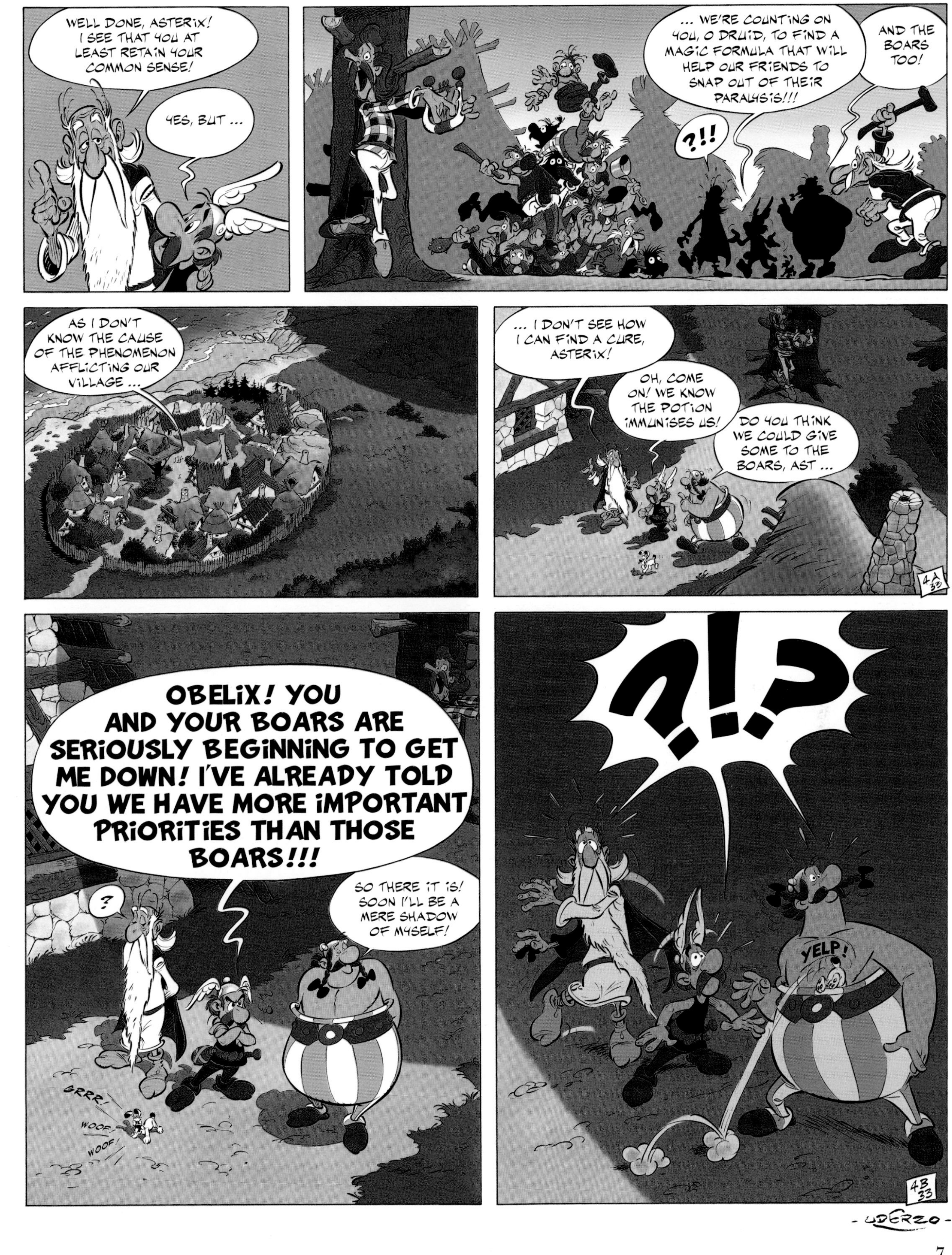
WELL DONE, ASTERIX! I SEE THAT YOU AT LEAST RETAIN YOUR COMMON SENSE!
YES, BUT ...
... WE'RE COUNTING ON YOU, O DRUID, TO FIND A MAGIC FORMULA THAT WILL HELP OUR FRIENDS TO SNAP OUT OF THEIR PARALYSIS!!!
AND THE BOARS TOO!
?!!
AS I DON'T KNOW THE CAUSE OF THE PHENOMENON AFFLICTING OUR VILLAGE ...
... I DON'T SEE HOW I CAN FIND A CURE, ASTERIX!
OH, COME ON! WE KNOW THE POTION IMMUNISES US!
DO YOU THINK WE COULD GIVE SOME TO THE BOARS, AST ...
OBELIX! YOU AND YOUR BOARS ARE SERIOUSLY BEGINNING TO GET ME DOWN! I'VE ALREADY TOLD YOU WE HAVE MORE IMPORTANT PRIORITIES THAN THOSE BOARS!!!
?
SO THERE IT IS! SOON I'LL BE A MERE SHADOW OF MYSELF!
GRRR!
WOOF!
WOOF!
?!?
YELP!
UDERZO

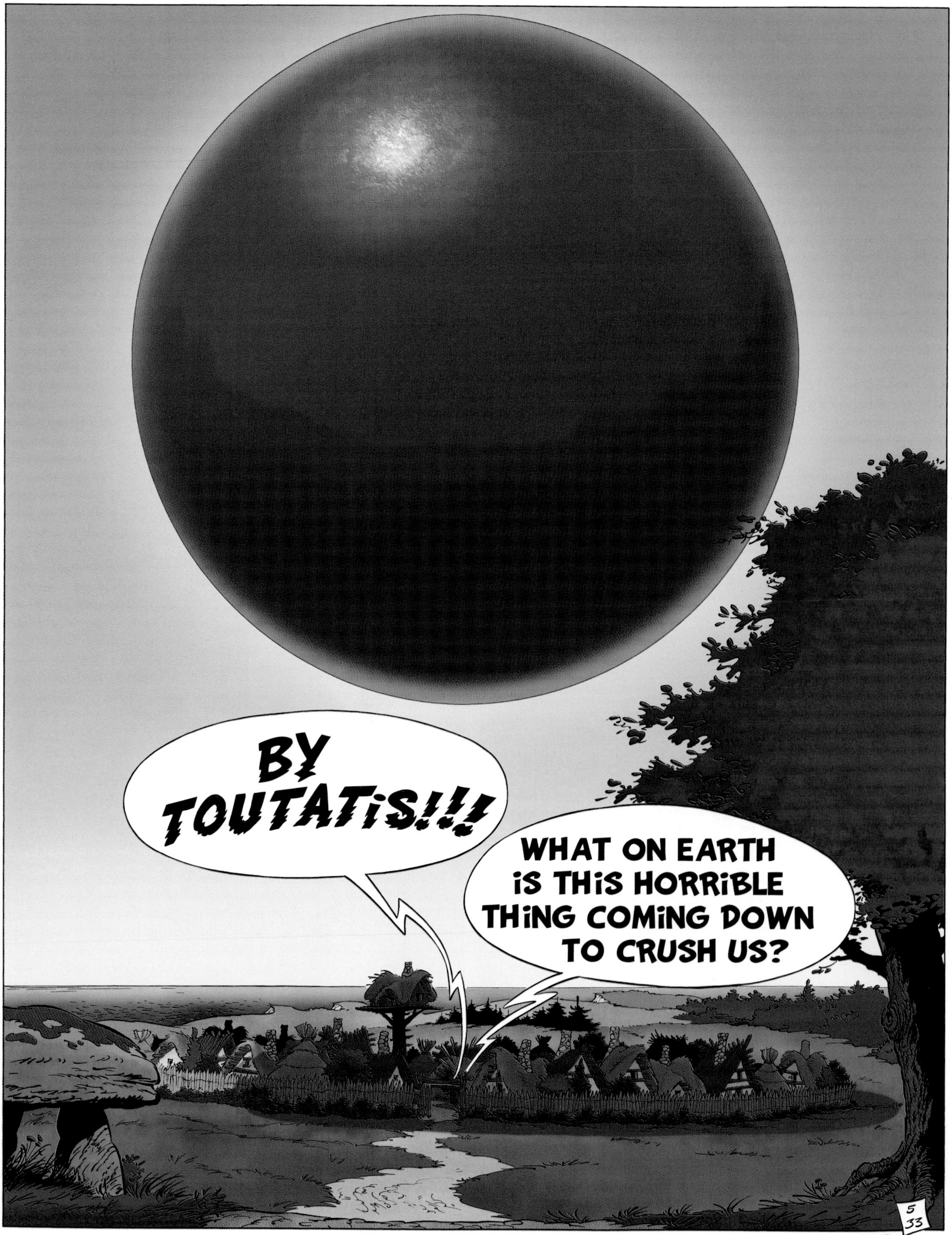
BY TOUTATIS!!!
WHAT ON EARTH IS THIS HORRIBLE THING COMING DOWN TO CRUSH US?
5 33
UDERZO

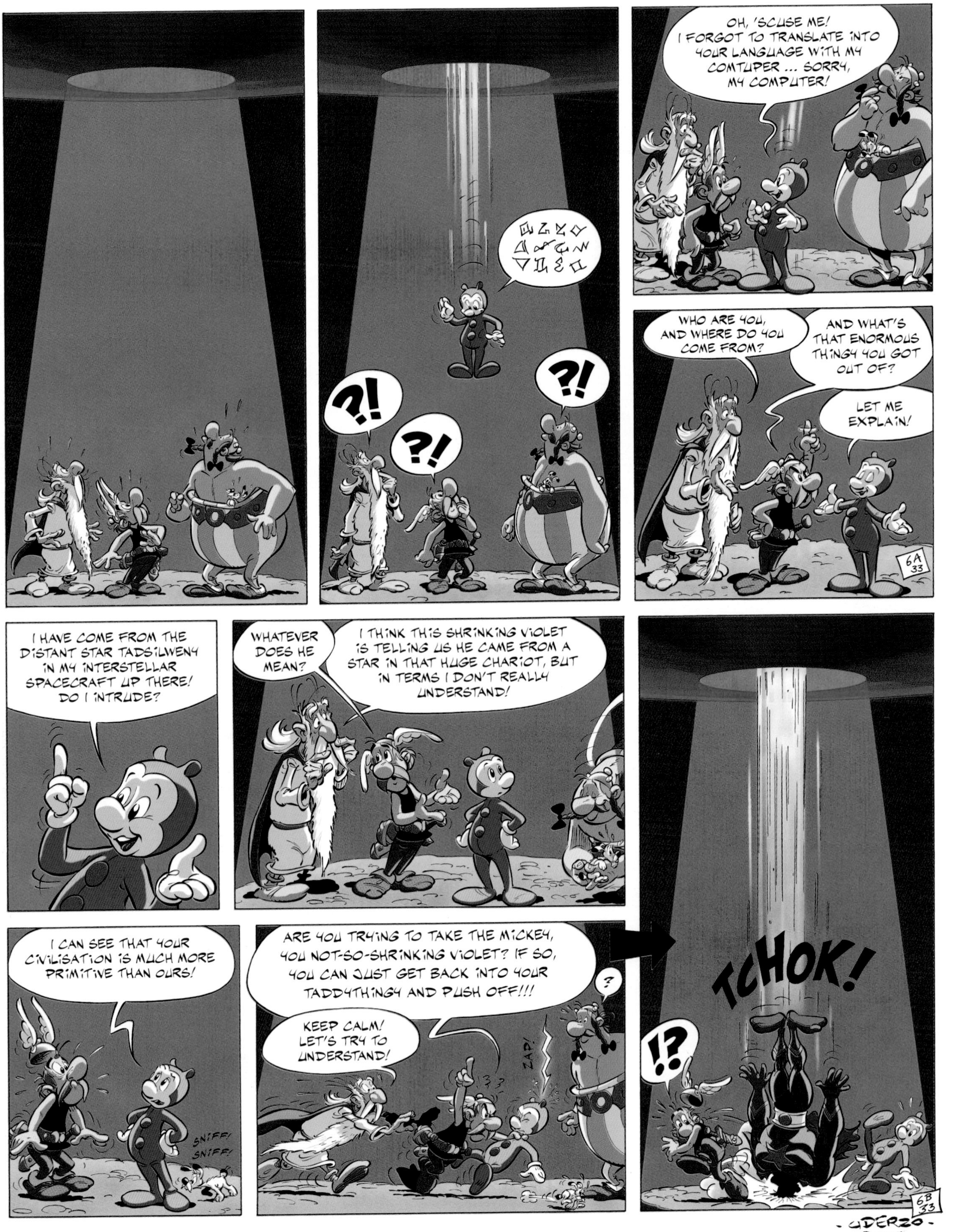
?!
?!
?!
OH, 'SCUSE ME! I FORGOT TO TRANSLATE INTO YOUR LANGUAGE WITH MY COMTUPER ... SORRY, MY COMPUTER!
WHO ARE YOU, AND WHERE DO YOU COME FROM?
AND WHAT'S THAT ENORMOUS THINGY YOU GOT OUT OF?
LET ME EXPLAIN!
I HAVE COME FROM THE DISTANT STAR TADSILWENY IN MY INTERSTELLAR SPACECRAFT UP THERE! DO I INTRUDE?
WHATEVER DOES HE MEAN?
I THINK THIS SHRINKING VIOLET IS TELLING US HE CAME FROM A STAR IN THAT HUGE CHARIOT, BUT IN TERMS I DON'T REALLY UNDERSTAND!
I CAN SEE THAT YOUR CIVILISATION IS MUCH MORE PRIMITIVE THAN OURS!
SNIFF! SNIFF!
ARE YOU TRYING TO TAKE THE MICKEY, YOU NOT-SO-SHRINKING VIOLET? IF SO, YOU CAN JUST GET BACK INTO YOUR TADDYTHINGY AND PUSH OFF!!!
?
KEEP CALM! LET'S TRY TO UNDERSTAND!
ZAP!
TCHOK!
!?
UDERZO

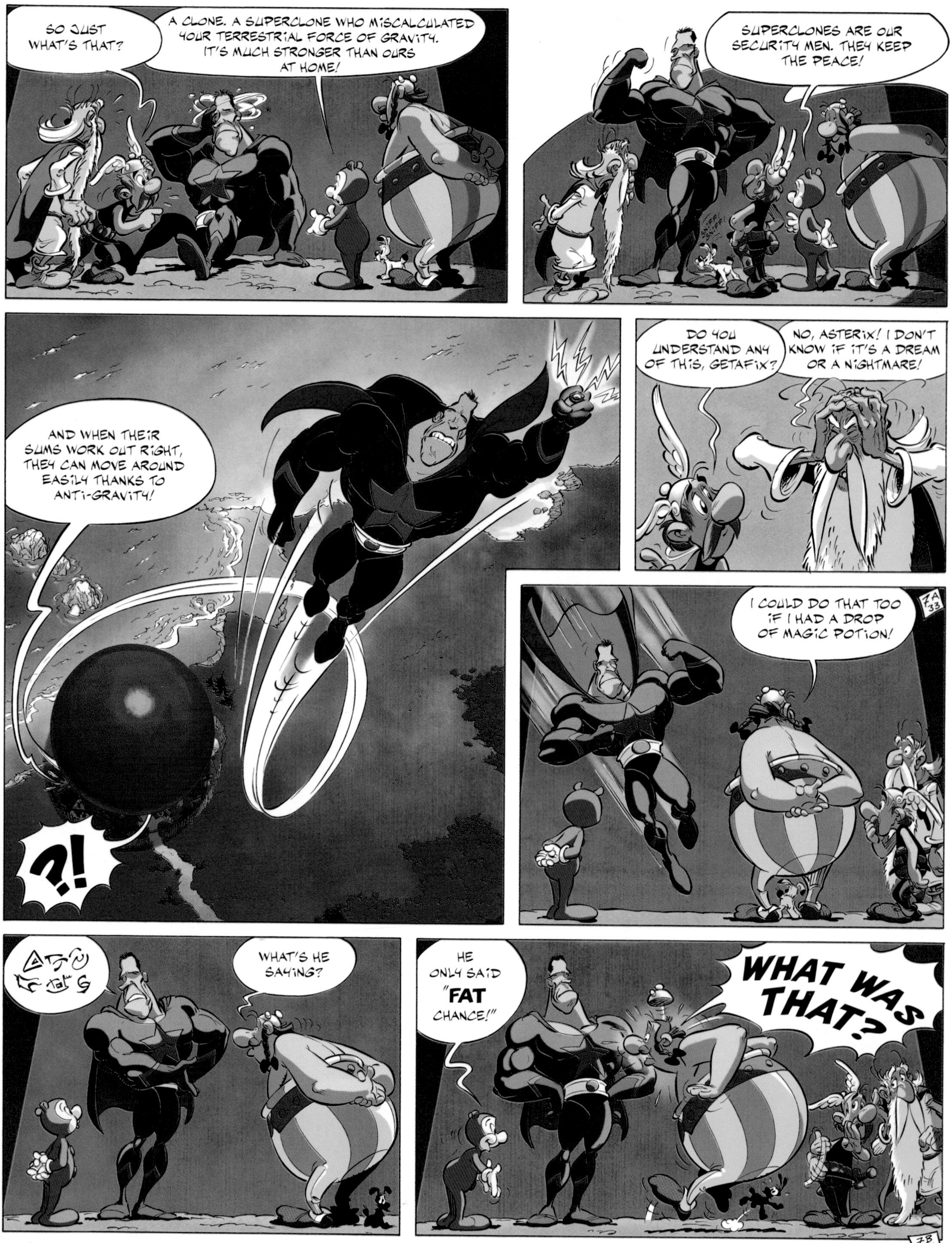
SO JUST WHAT'S THAT?
A CLONE. A SUPERCLONE WHO MISCALCULATED YOUR TERRESTRIAL FORCE OF GRAVITY. IT'S MUCH STRONGER THAN OURS AT HOME!
SUPERCLONES ARE OUR SECURITY MEN. THEY KEEP THE PEACE!
AND WHEN THEIR SUMS WORK OUT RIGHT, THEY CAN MOVE AROUND EASILY THANKS TO ANTI-GRAVITY!
?!
DO YOU UNDERSTAND ANY OF THIS, GETAFIX?
NO, ASTERIX! I DON'T KNOW IF IT'S A DREAM OR A NIGHTMARE!
I COULD DO THAT TOO IF I HAD A DROP OF MAGIC POTION!
WHAT'S HE SAYING?
HE ONLY SAID "FAT CHANCE!"
WHAT WAS THAT?
UDERZO

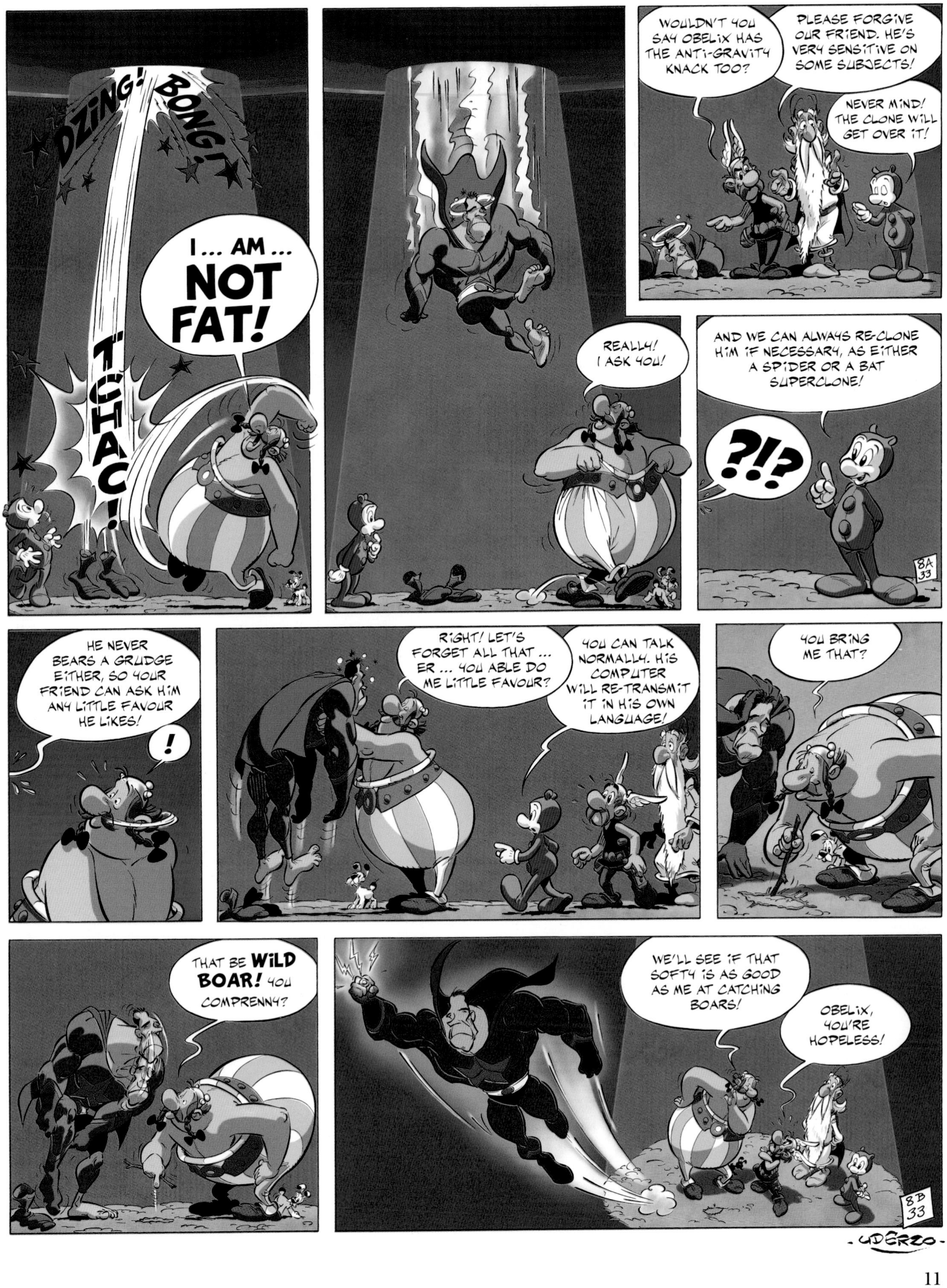
DZING! BONG! BONG!
I ... AM ... NOT FAT!
TCHAC!
WOULDN'T YOU SAY OBELIX HAS THE ANTI-GRAVITY KNACK TOO?
PLEASE FORGIVE OUR FRIEND. HE'S VERY SENSITIVE ON SOME SUBJECTS!
NEVER MIND! THE CLONE WILL GET OVER IT!
REALLY! I ASK YOU!
AND WE CAN ALWAYS RE-CLONE HIM IF NECESSARY, AS EITHER A SPIDER OR A BAT SUPERCLONE!
?!?
8A 33
HE NEVER BEARS A GRUDGE EITHER, SO YOUR FRIEND CAN ASK HIM ANY LITTLE FAVOUR HE LIKES!
!
RIGHT! LET'S FORGET ALL THAT ... ER ... YOU ABLE DO ME LITTLE FAVOUR?
YOU CAN TALK NORMALLY. HIS COMPUTER WILL RE-TRANSMIT IT IN HIS OWN LANGUAGE!
YOU BRING ME THAT?
THAT BE WILD BOAR! YOU COMPRENNY?
WE'LL SEE IF THAT SOFTY IS AS GOOD AS ME AT CATCHING BOARS!
OBELIX, YOU'RE HOPELESS!
8B 33
UDERZO

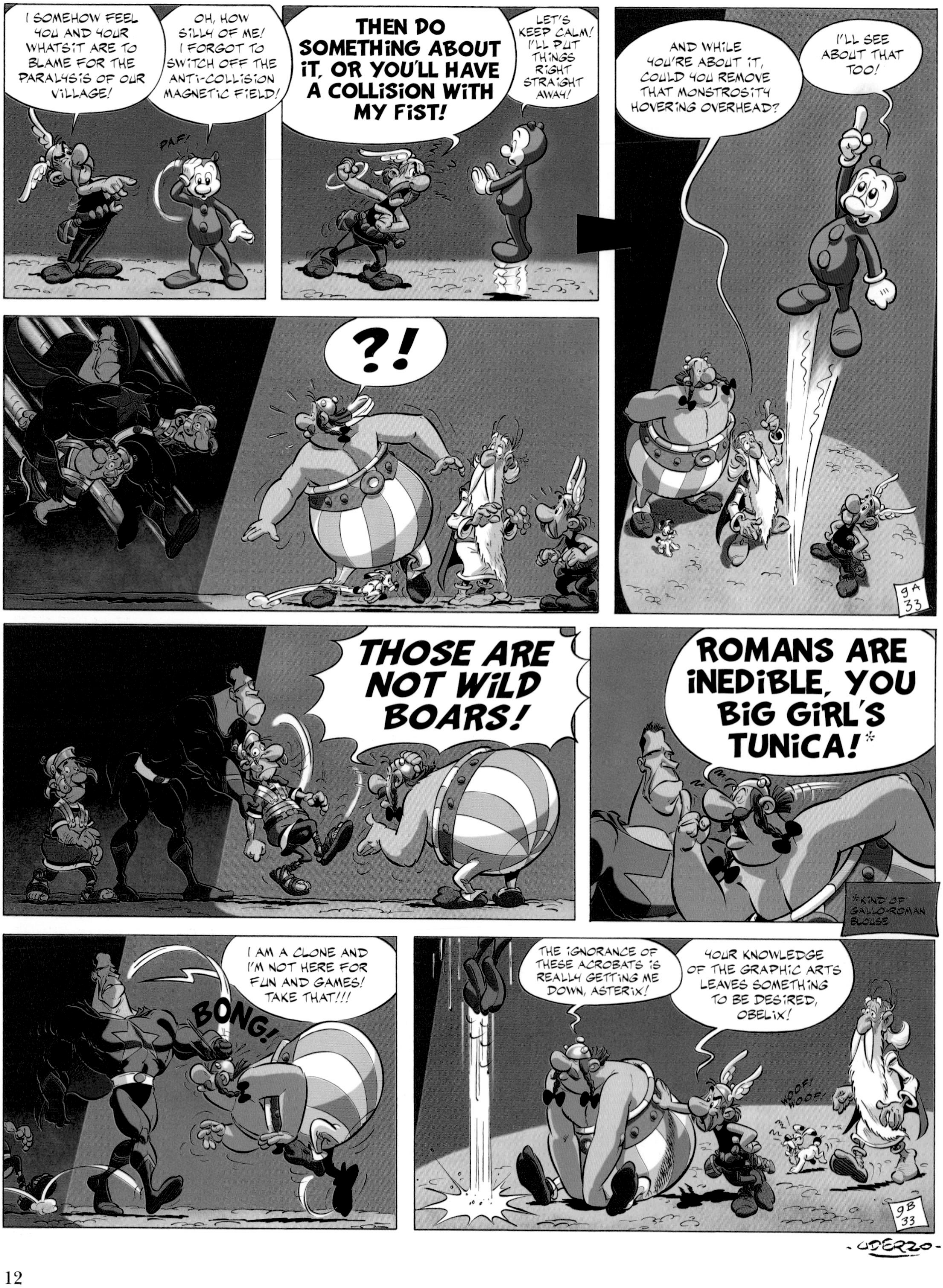
I SOMEHOW FEEL YOU AND YOUR WHATSIT ARE TO BLAME FOR THE PARALYSIS OF OUR VILLAGE!
OH, HOW SILLY OF ME! I FORGOT TO SWITCH OFF THE ANTI-COLLISION MAGNETIC FIELD!
PAF!
THEN DO SOMETHING ABOUT IT, OR YOU'LL HAVE A COLLISION WITH MY FIST!
LET'S KEEP CALM! I'LL PUT THINGS RIGHT STRAIGHT AWAY!
AND WHILE YOU'RE ABOUT IT, COULD YOU REMOVE THAT MONSTROSITY HOVERING OVERHEAD?
I'LL SEE ABOUT THAT TOO!
?!
9A 33
THOSE ARE NOT WILD BOARS!
ROMANS ARE INEDIBLE, YOU BIG GIRL'S TUNICA!*
*KIND OF GALLO-ROMAN BLOUSE
I AM A CLONE AND I'M NOT HERE FOR FUN AND GAMES! TAKE THAT!!!
BONG!
THE IGNORANCE OF THESE ACROBATS IS REALLY GETTING ME DOWN, ASTERIX!
YOUR KNOWLEDGE OF THE GRAPHIC ARTS LEAVES SOMETHING TO BE DESIRED, OBELIX!
WOOF! WOOF!
9B 33
UDERZO

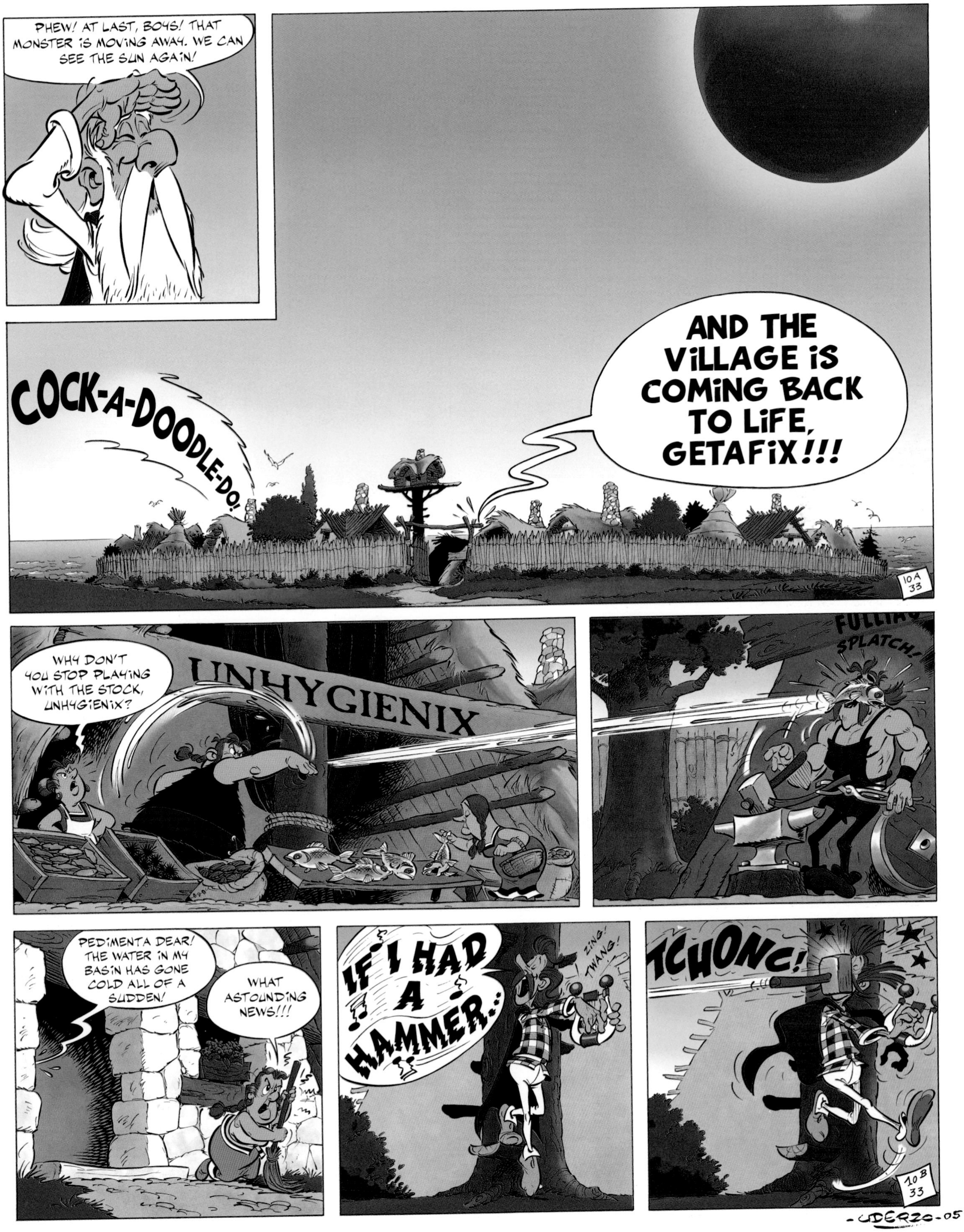

PHEW! AT LAST, BOYS! THAT MONSTER IS MOVING AWAY. WE CAN SEE THE SUN AGAIN!
COCK-A-DOODLE-DO!
AND THE VILLAGE IS COMING BACK TO LIFE, GETAFIX!!!
10 A 33
UNHYGIENIX
WHY DON'T YOU STOP PLAYING WITH THE STOCK, UNHYGIENIX?
SPLATCH!
PEDIMENTA DEAR! THE WATER IN MY BASIN HAS GONE COLD ALL OF A SUDDEN!
WHAT ASTOUNDING NEWS!!!
IF I HAD A HAMMER...
ZING! TWANG!
TCHONC!
10 B 33
-UDERZO-05

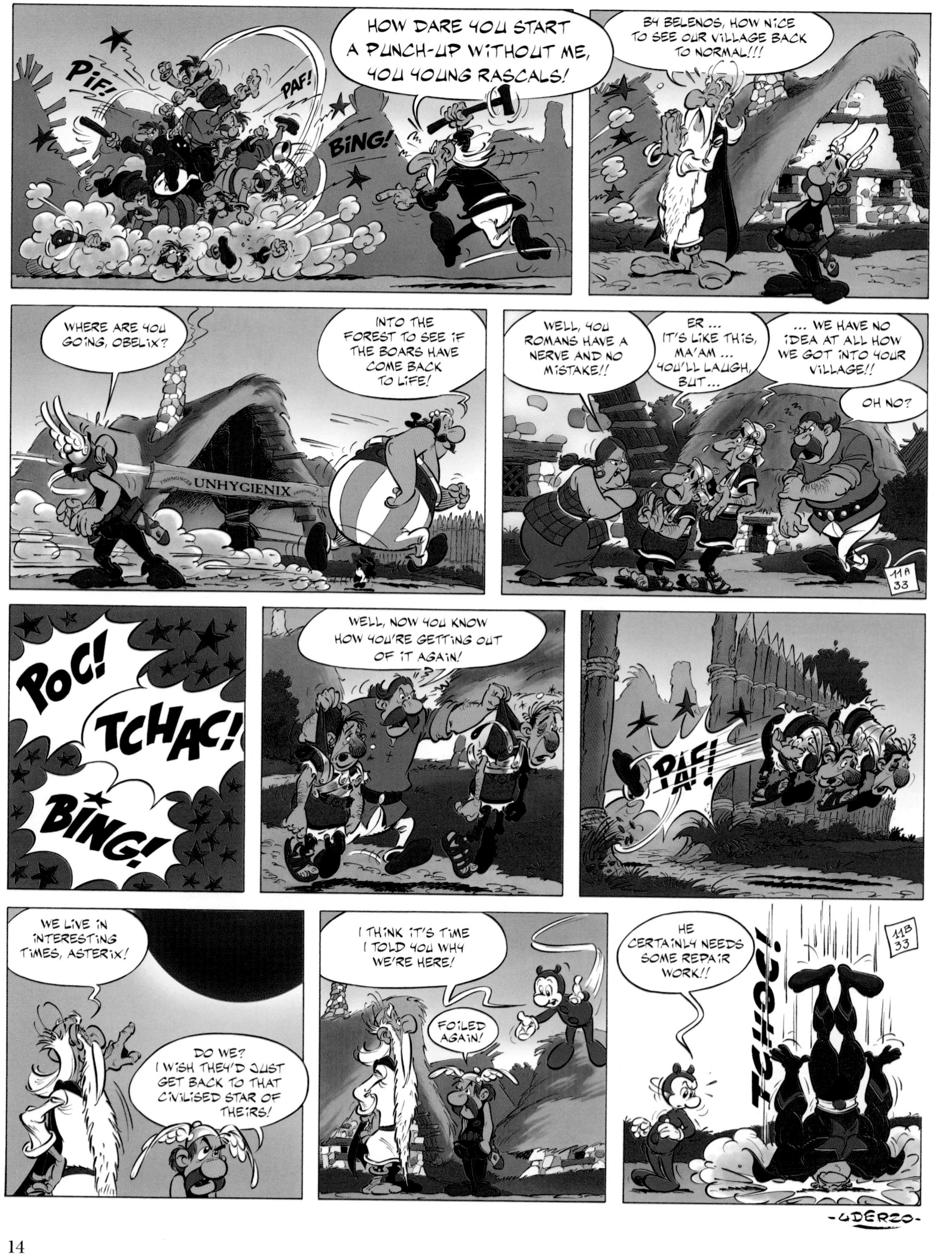
PIF!
PAF!
BING!
HOW DARE YOU START A PUNCH-UP WITHOUT ME, YOU YOUNG RASCALS!
BY BELENOS, HOW NICE TO SEE OUR VILLAGE BACK TO NORMAL!!!
WHERE ARE YOU GOING, OBELIX?
INTO THE FOREST TO SEE IF THE BOARS HAVE COME BACK TO LIFE!
FISHMONGER UNHYGIENIX FISHMONGER
WELL, YOU ROMANS HAVE A NERVE AND NO MISTAKE!!
ER ... IT'S LIKE THIS, MA'AM ... YOU'LL LAUGH, BUT ...
... WE HAVE NO IDEA AT ALL HOW WE GOT INTO YOUR VILLAGE!!
OH NO?
11A 33
POC!
TCHAC!
BING!
WELL, NOW YOU KNOW HOW YOU'RE GETTING OUT OF IT AGAIN!
PAF!
WE LIVE IN INTERESTING TIMES, ASTERIX!
DO WE? I WISH THEY'D JUST GET BACK TO THAT CIVILISED STAR OF THEIRS!
I THINK IT'S TIME I TOLD YOU WHY WE'RE HERE!
FOILED AGAIN!
HE CERTAINLY NEEDS SOME REPAIR WORK!!
TCHAC!
11B 33
-UDERZO-

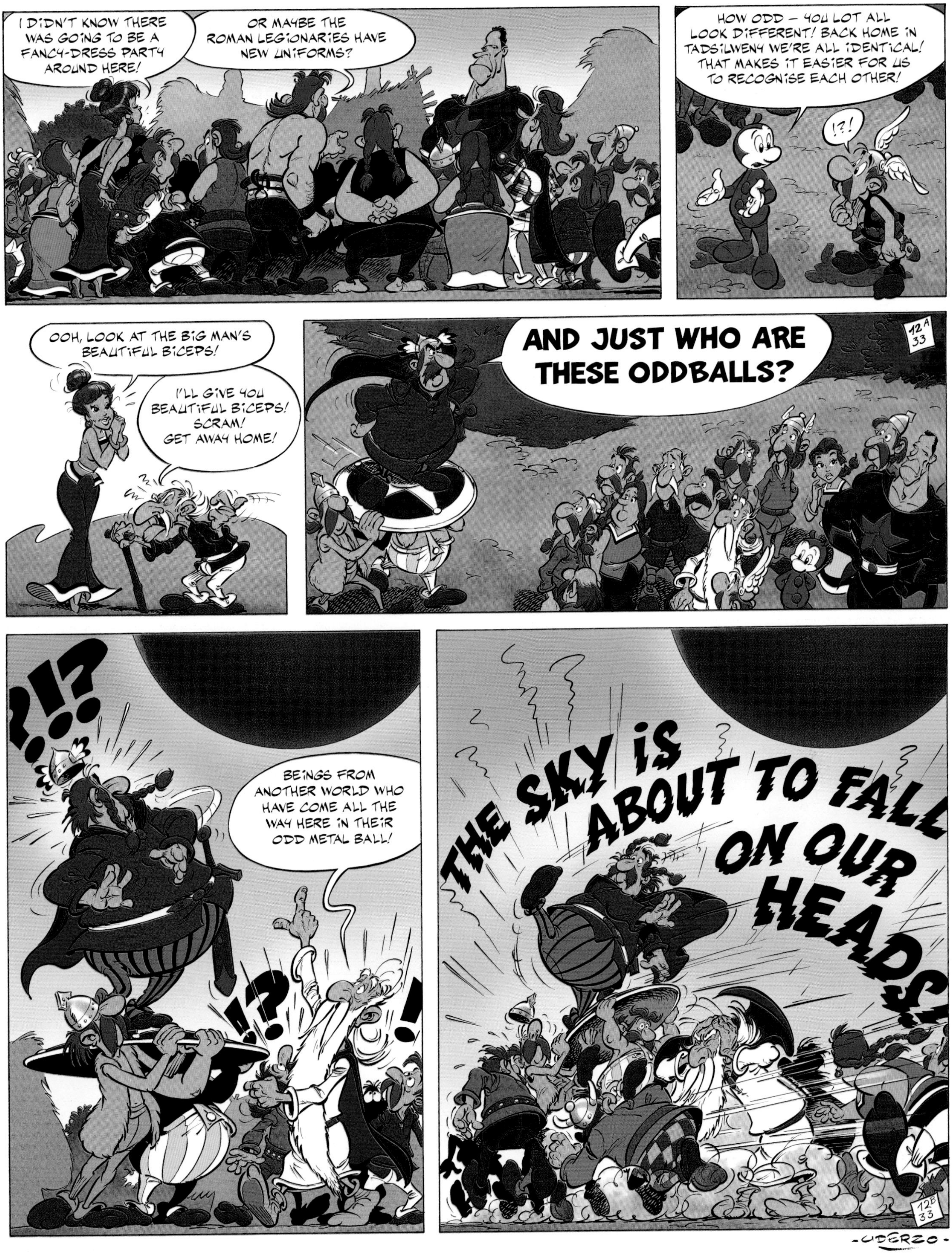

I DIDN'T KNOW THERE WAS GOING TO BE A FANCY-DRESS PARTY AROUND HERE!
OR MAYBE THE ROMAN LEGIONARIES HAVE NEW UNIFORMS?
HOW ODD – YOU LOT ALL LOOK DIFFERENT! BACK HOME IN TADSILWENY WE'RE ALL IDENTICAL! THAT MAKES IT EASIER FOR US TO RECOGNISE EACH OTHER!
!?!
OOH, LOOK AT THE BIG MAN'S BEAUTIFUL BICEPS!
I'LL GIVE YOU BEAUTIFUL BICEPS! SCRAM! GET AWAY HOME!
AND JUST WHO ARE THESE ODDBALLS?
12A 33
?!?...
BEINGS FROM ANOTHER WORLD WHO HAVE COME ALL THE WAY HERE IN THEIR ODD METAL BALL!
!?!
THE SKY IS ABOUT TO FALL ON OUR HEADS!
12B 33
UDERZO

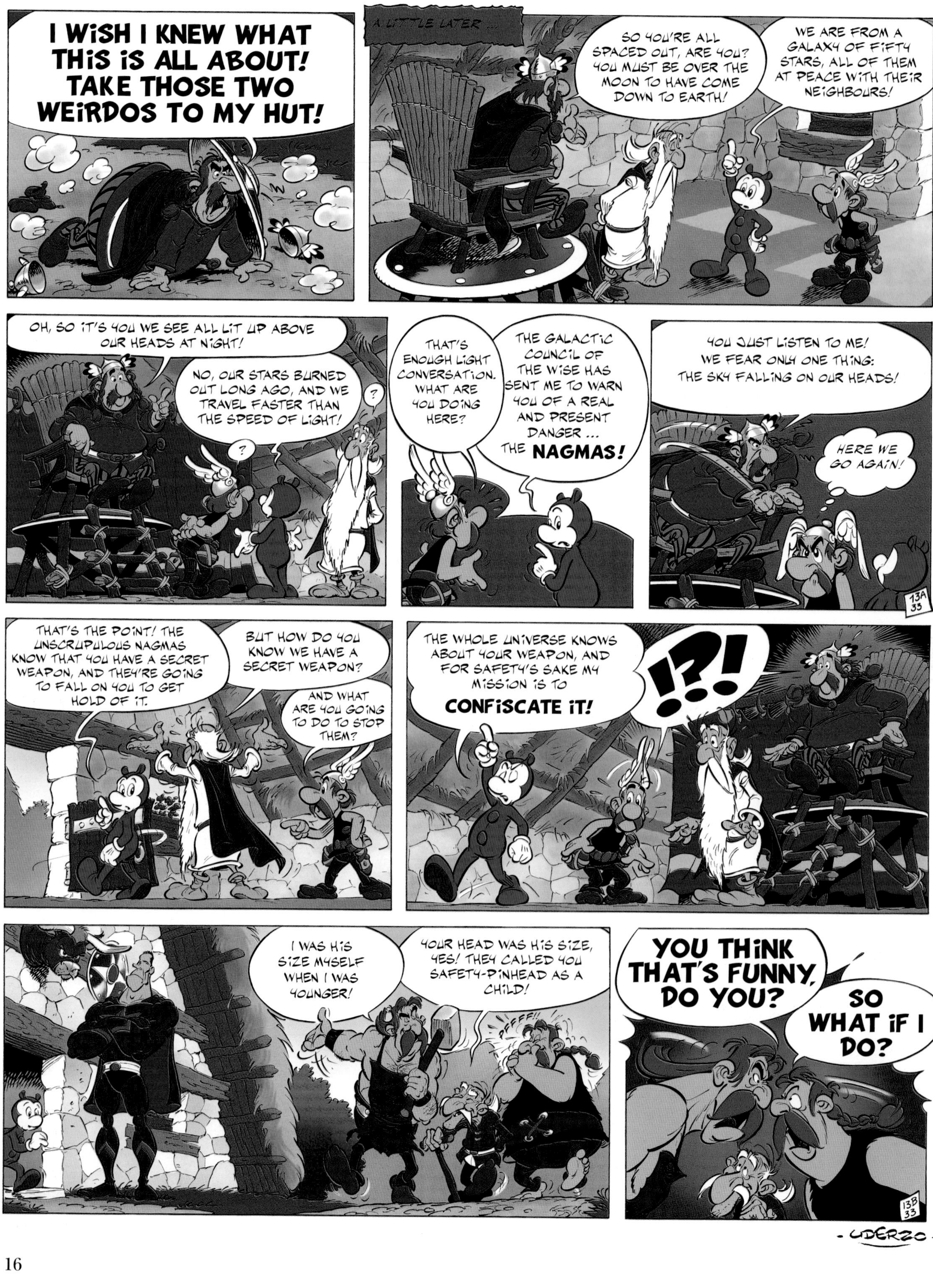
I WISH I KNEW WHAT THIS IS ALL ABOUT! TAKE THOSE TWO WEIRDOS TO MY HUT!
A LITTLE LATER ...
SO YOU'RE ALL SPACED OUT, ARE YOU? YOU MUST BE OVER THE MOON TO HAVE COME DOWN TO EARTH!
WE ARE FROM A GALAXY OF FIFTY STARS, ALL OF THEM AT PEACE WITH THEIR NEIGHBOURS!
OH, SO IT'S YOU WE SEE ALL LIT UP ABOVE OUR HEADS AT NIGHT!
NO, OUR STARS BURNED OUT LONG AGO, AND WE TRAVEL FASTER THAN THE SPEED OF LIGHT!
?
?
THAT'S ENOUGH LIGHT CONVERSATION. WHAT ARE YOU DOING HERE?
THE GALACTIC COUNCIL OF THE WISE HAS SENT ME TO WARN YOU OF A REAL AND PRESENT DANGER ... THE NAGMAS!
YOU JUST LISTEN TO ME! WE FEAR ONLY ONE THING: THE SKY FALLING ON OUR HEADS!
HERE WE GO AGAIN!
THAT'S THE POINT! THE UNSCRUPULOUS NAGMAS KNOW THAT YOU HAVE A SECRET WEAPON, AND THEY'RE GOING TO FALL ON YOU TO GET HOLD OF IT.
BUT HOW DO YOU KNOW WE HAVE A SECRET WEAPON?
AND WHAT ARE YOU GOING TO DO TO STOP THEM?
THE WHOLE UNIVERSE KNOWS ABOUT YOUR WEAPON, AND FOR SAFETY'S SAKE MY MISSION IS TO CONFISCATE IT!
!?!
I WAS HIS SIZE MYSELF WHEN I WAS YOUNGER!
YOUR HEAD WAS HIS SIZE, YES! THEY CALLED YOU SAFETY-PINHEAD AS A CHILD!
YOU THINK THAT'S FUNNY, DO YOU?
SO WHAT IF I DO?
UDERZO

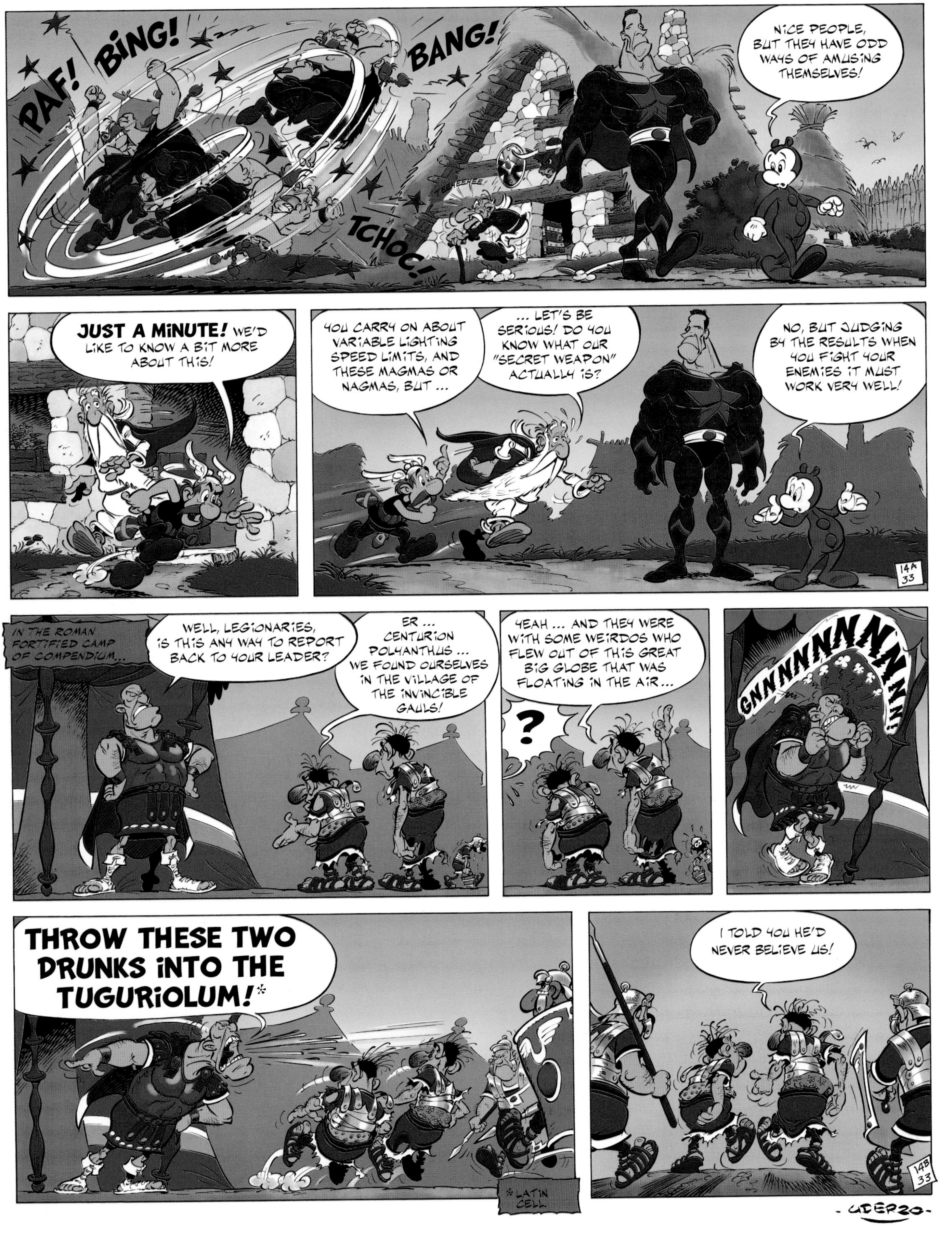
PAF!
BING!
BANG!
TCHOC!
NICE PEOPLE, BUT THEY HAVE ODD WAYS OF AMUSING THEMSELVES!
JUST A MINUTE! WE'D LIKE TO KNOW A BIT MORE ABOUT THIS!
YOU CARRY ON ABOUT VARIABLE LIGHTING SPEED LIMITS, AND THESE MAGMAS OR NAGMAS, BUT ...
... LET'S BE SERIOUS! DO YOU KNOW WHAT OUR "SECRET WEAPON" ACTUALLY IS?
NO, BUT JUDGING BY THE RESULTS WHEN YOU FIGHT YOUR ENEMIES IT MUST WORK VERY WELL!
IN THE ROMAN FORTIFIED CAMP OF COMPENDIUM...
WELL, LEGIONARIES, IS THIS ANY WAY TO REPORT BACK TO YOUR LEADER?
ER ... CENTURION POLYANTHUS ... WE FOUND OURSELVES IN THE VILLAGE OF THE INVINCIBLE GAULS!
?
YEAH ... AND THEY WERE WITH SOME WEIRDOS WHO FLEW OUT OF THIS GREAT BIG GLOBE THAT WAS FLOATING IN THE AIR...
GNNNNNNNNNNN!
THROW THESE TWO DRUNKS INTO THE TUGURIOLUM!*
*LATIN CELL.
I TOLD YOU HE'D NEVER BELIEVE US!
UDERZO

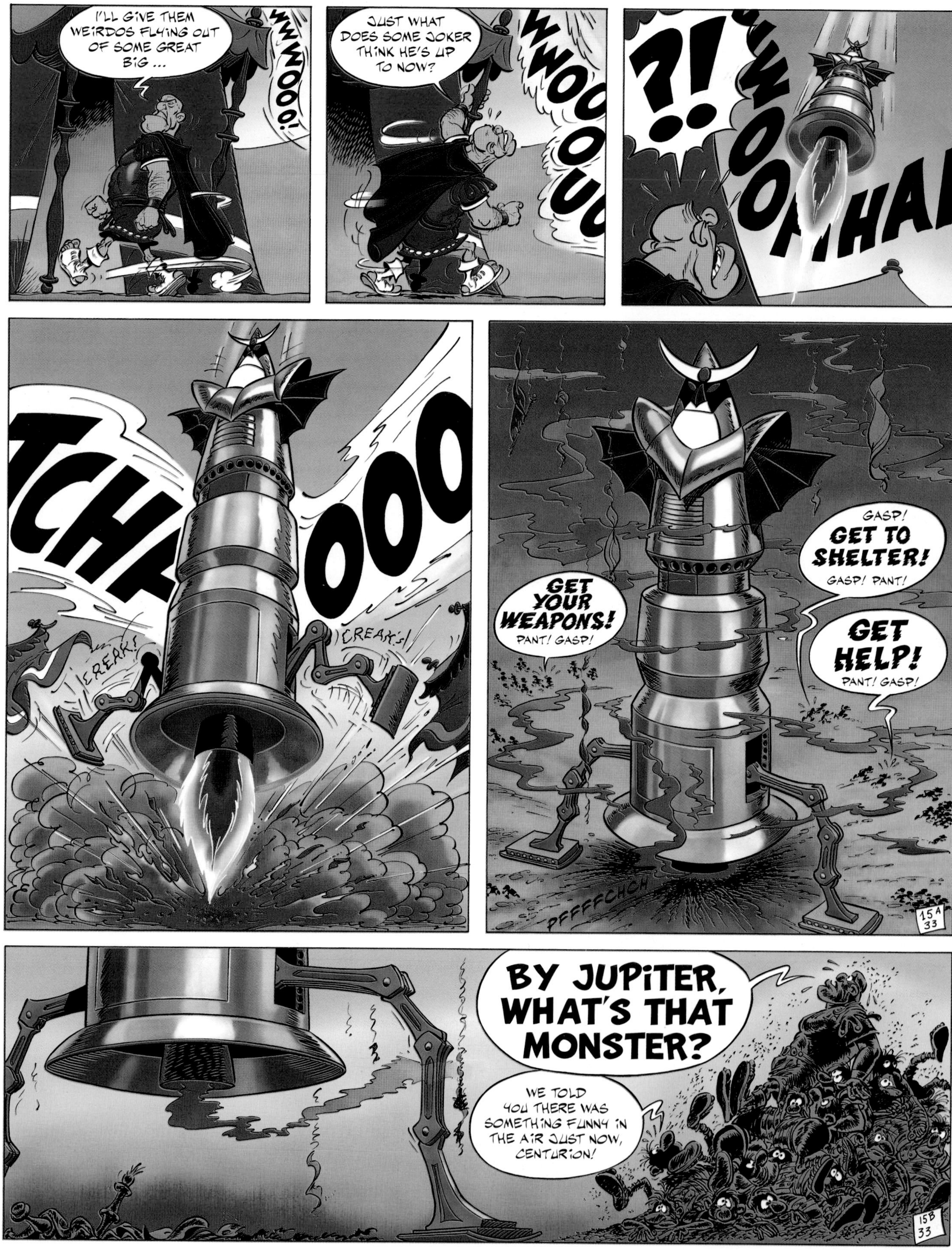
I'LL GIVE THEM WEIRDOS FLYING OUT OF SOME GREAT BIG ...
WWWOOOO!
JUST WHAT DOES SOME JOKER THINK HE'S UP TO NOW?
WWOOOOUU
?!!
TCHHOOO
CREAK!
CREAK!
GET YOUR WEAPONS! PANT! GASP!
GASP! GET TO SHELTER! GASP! PANT!
GET HELP! PANT! GASP!
PFFFFCHCH
BY JUPITER, WHAT'S THAT MONSTER?
WE TOLD YOU THERE WAS SOMETHING FUNNY IN THE AIR JUST NOW, CENTURION!
UDERZO

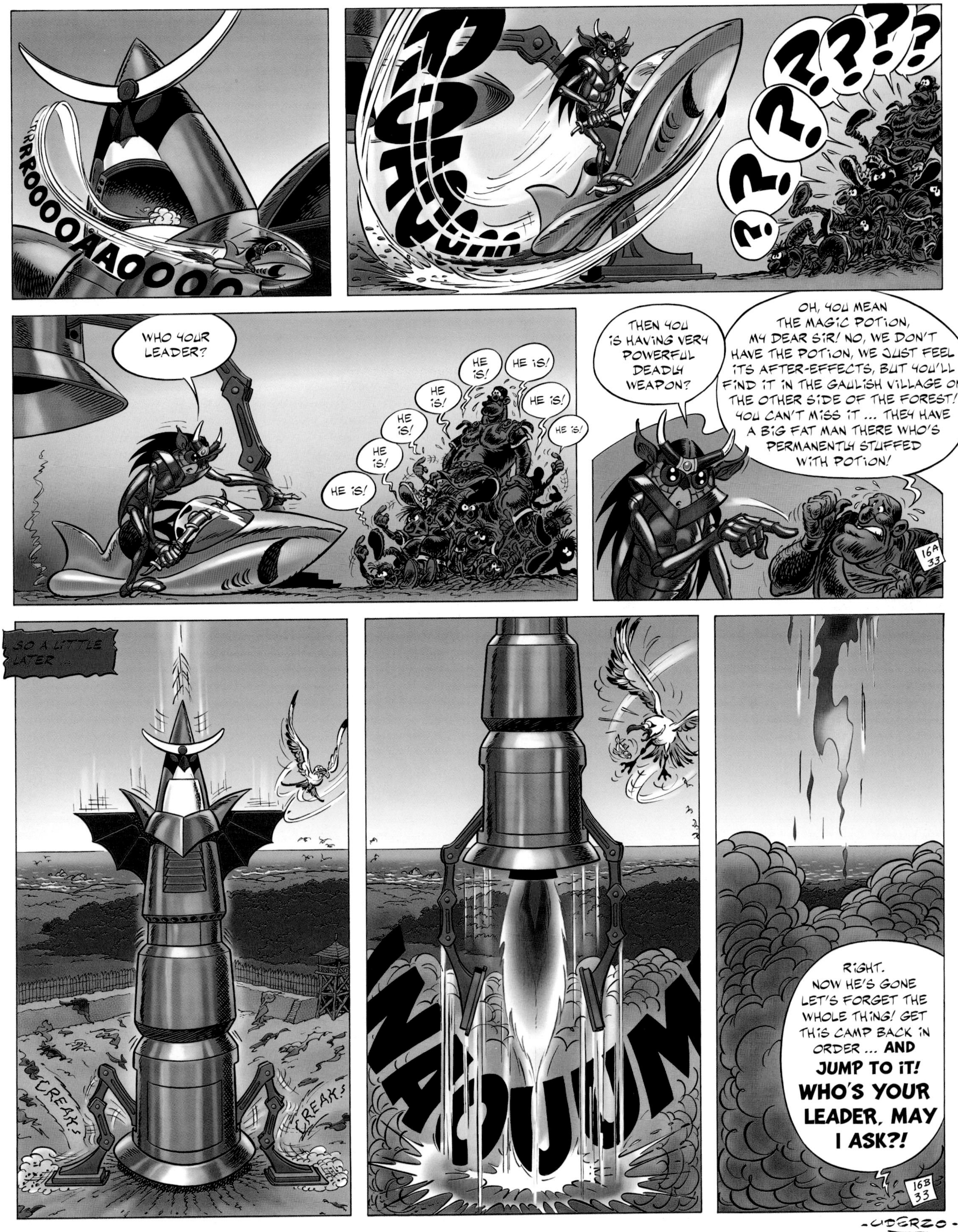

WHO YOUR LEADER?
HE IS!
HE IS!
HE IS!
HE IS!
HE IS!
HE IS!
HE IS!
HE IS!
THEN YOU IS HAVING VERY POWERFUL DEADLY WEAPON?
OH, YOU MEAN THE MAGIC POTION, MY DEAR SIR! NO, WE DON'T HAVE THE POTION, WE JUST FEEL ITS AFTER-EFFECTS, BUT YOU'LL FIND IT IN THE GAULISH VILLAGE ON THE OTHER SIDE OF THE FOREST! YOU CAN'T MISS IT ... THEY HAVE A BIG FAT MAN THERE WHO'S PERMANENTLY STUFFED WITH POTION!
16A 33
SO A LITTLE LATER ...
CREAK!
CREAK!
RIGHT. NOW HE'S GONE LET'S FORGET THE WHOLE THING! GET THIS CAMP BACK IN ORDER ... AND JUMP TO IT! WHO'S YOUR LEADER, MAY I ASK?!
16B 33
UDERZO

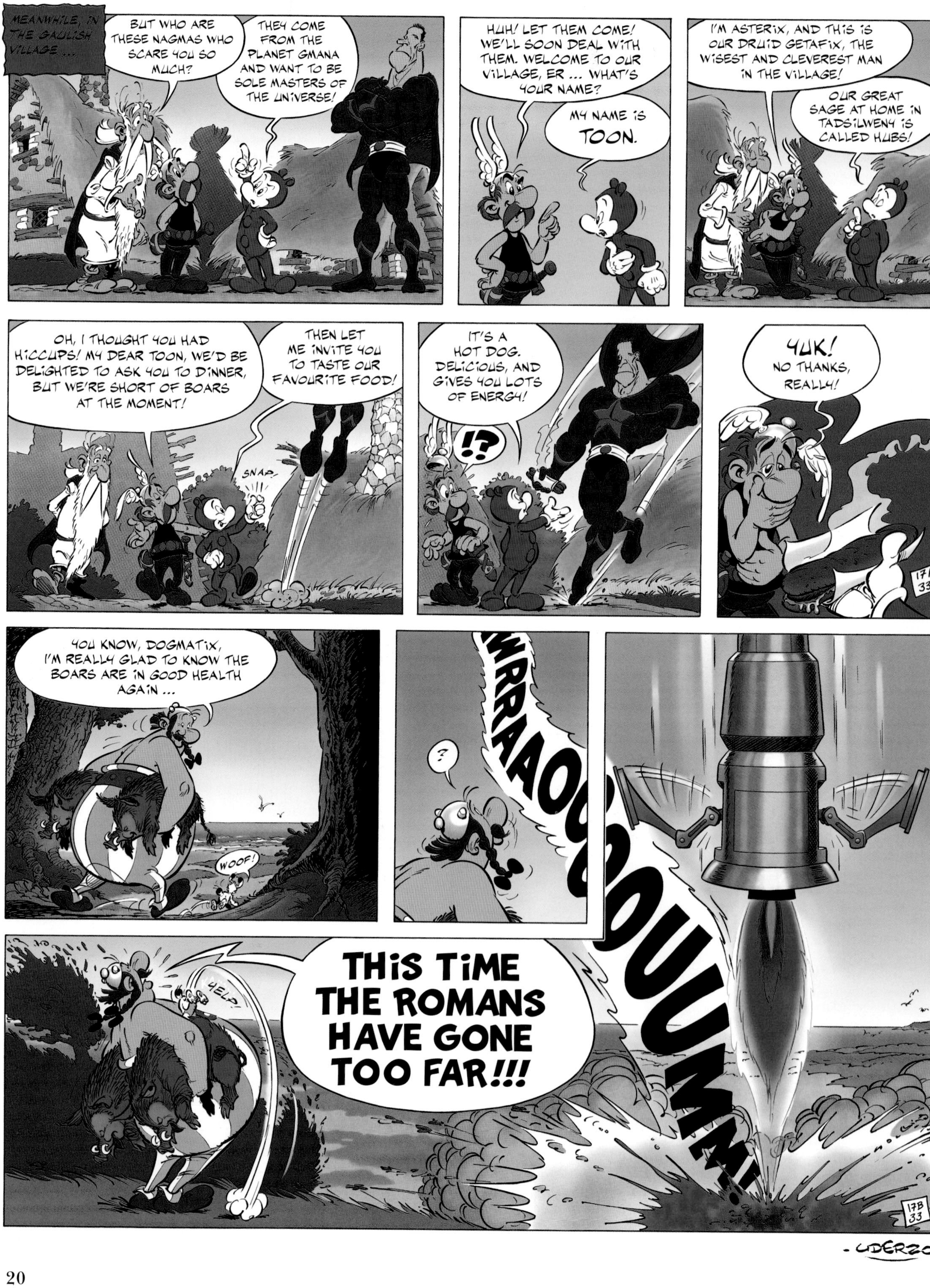
MEANWHILE, IN THE GAULISH VILLAGE ...
BUT WHO ARE THESE NAGMAS WHO SCARE YOU SO MUCH?
THEY COME FROM THE PLANET GMANA AND WANT TO BE SOLE MASTERS OF THE UNIVERSE!
HUH! LET THEM COME! WE'LL SOON DEAL WITH THEM. WELCOME TO OUR VILLAGE, ER ... WHAT'S YOUR NAME?
MY NAME IS TOON.
I'M ASTERIX, AND THIS IS OUR DRUID GETAFIX, THE WISEST AND CLEVEREST MAN IN THE VILLAGE!
OUR GREAT SAGE AT HOME IN TADSILWENY IS CALLED HUBS!
OH, I THOUGHT YOU HAD HICCUPS! MY DEAR TOON, WE'D BE DELIGHTED TO ASK YOU TO DINNER, BUT WE'RE SHORT OF BOARS AT THE MOMENT!
THEN LET ME INVITE YOU TO TASTE OUR FAVOURITE FOOD!
SNAP!
IT'S A HOT DOG. DELICIOUS, AND GIVES YOU LOTS OF ENERGY!
!?
YUK! NO THANKS, REALLY!
17A 33
YOU KNOW, DOGMATIX, I'M REALLY GLAD TO KNOW THE BOARS ARE IN GOOD HEALTH AGAIN ...
WOOF!
?
VRRRAAOOOOOOUUMM!
HELP!
THIS TIME THE ROMANS HAVE GONE TOO FAR!!!
17B 33
UDERZO

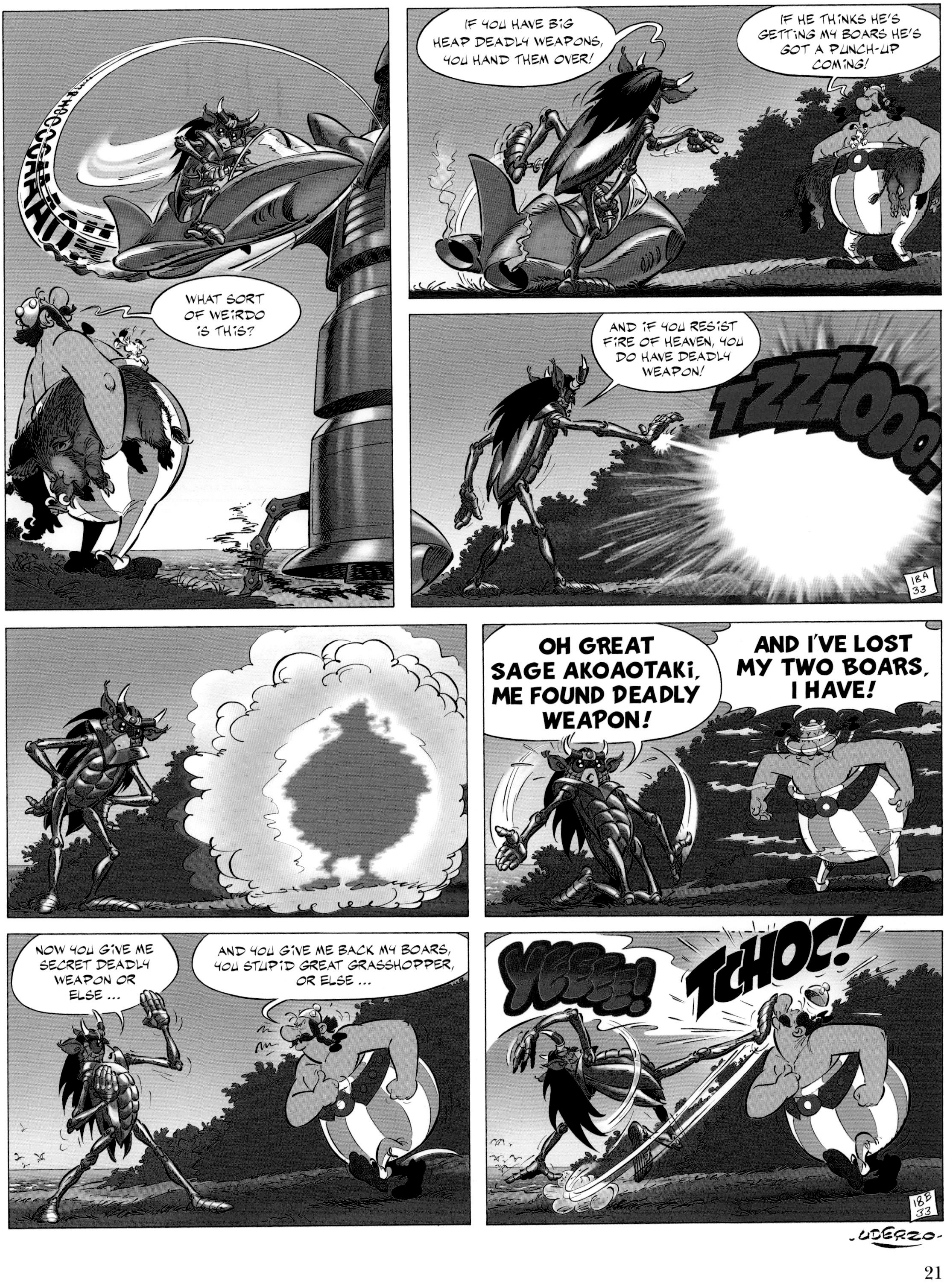
WHAT SORT OF WEIRDO IS THIS?
IF YOU HAVE BIG HEAP DEADLY WEAPONS, YOU HAND THEM OVER!
IF HE THINKS HE'S GETTING MY BOARS HE'S GOT A PUNCH-UP COMING!
AND IF YOU RESIST FIRE OF HEAVEN, YOU DO HAVE DEADLY WEAPON!
TZZIOOO...
OH GREAT SAGE AKOAOTAKI, ME FOUND DEADLY WEAPON!
AND I'VE LOST MY TWO BOARS, I HAVE!
NOW YOU GIVE ME SECRET DEADLY WEAPON OR ELSE ...
AND YOU GIVE ME BACK MY BOARS, YOU STUPID GREAT GRASSHOPPER, OR ELSE ...
YEEEE!
TCHOC!
UDERZO

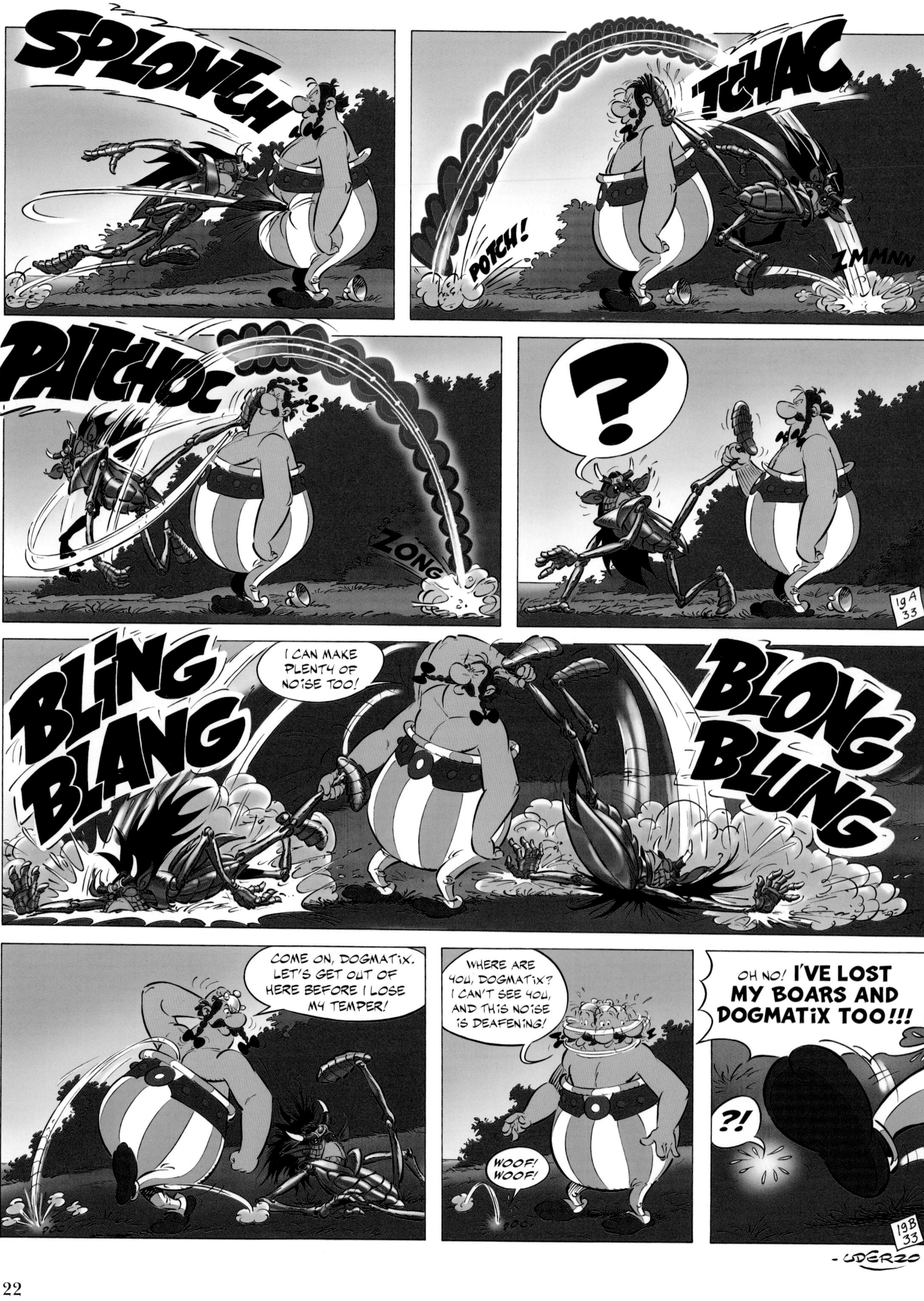
SPLONTCH
TCHAC
POTCH!
ZMMNN
PATCHOC
ZONG
?
19A 33
BLING BLANG
I CAN MAKE PLENTY OF NOISE TOO!
BLONG BLUNG
COME ON, DOGMATIX. LET'S GET OUT OF HERE BEFORE I LOSE MY TEMPER!
POC
WHERE ARE YOU, DOGMATIX? I CAN'T SEE YOU, AND THIS NOISE IS DEAFENING!
WOOF! WOOF!
POC
OH NO! I'VE LOST MY BOARS AND DOGMATIX TOO!!!
?!
19B 33
- UDERZO -

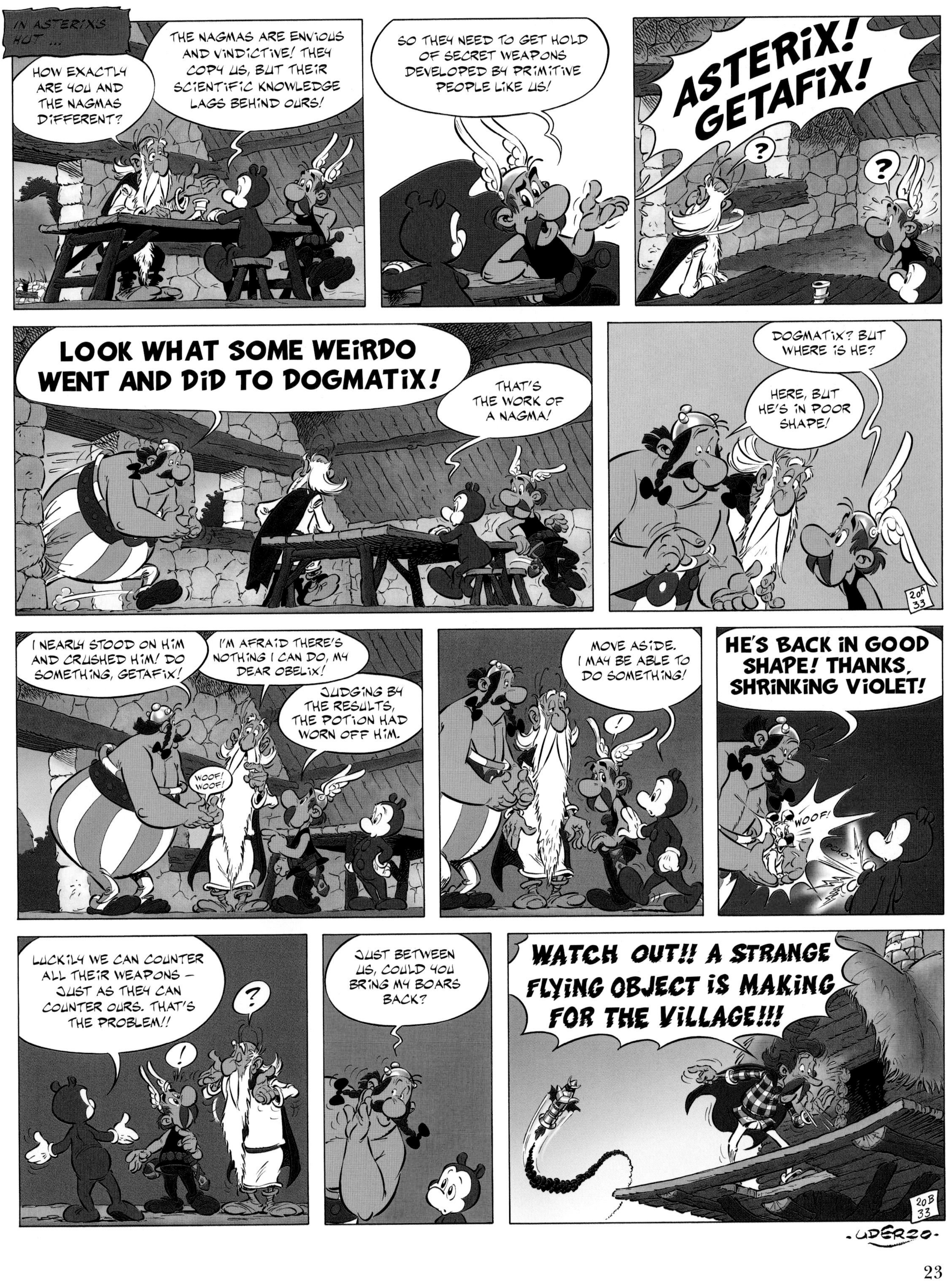
IN ASTERIX'S HUT ...
HOW EXACTLY ARE YOU AND THE NAGMAS DIFFERENT?
THE NAGMAS ARE ENVIOUS AND VINDICTIVE! THEY COPY US, BUT THEIR SCIENTIFIC KNOWLEDGE LAGS BEHIND OURS!
SO THEY NEED TO GET HOLD OF SECRET WEAPONS DEVELOPED BY PRIMITIVE PEOPLE LIKE US!
ASTERIX! GETAFIX!
?
?
LOOK WHAT SOME WEIRDO WENT AND DID TO DOGMATIX!
THAT'S THE WORK OF A NAGMA!
DOGMATIX? BUT WHERE IS HE?
HERE, BUT HE'S IN POOR SHAPE!
I NEARLY STOOD ON HIM AND CRUSHED HIM! DO SOMETHING, GETAFIX!
I'M AFRAID THERE'S NOTHING I CAN DO, MY DEAR OBELIX!
JUDGING BY THE RESULTS, THE POTION HAD WORN OFF HIM.
WOOF! WOOF!
MOVE ASIDE. I MAY BE ABLE TO DO SOMETHING!
!
HE'S BACK IN GOOD SHAPE! THANKS, SHRINKING VIOLET!
WOOF!
LUCKILY WE CAN COUNTER ALL THEIR WEAPONS – JUST AS THEY CAN COUNTER OURS. THAT'S THE PROBLEM!!
?
!
JUST BETWEEN US, COULD YOU BRING MY BOARS BACK?
WATCH OUT!! A STRANGE FLYING OBJECT IS MAKING FOR THE VILLAGE!!!
UDERZO

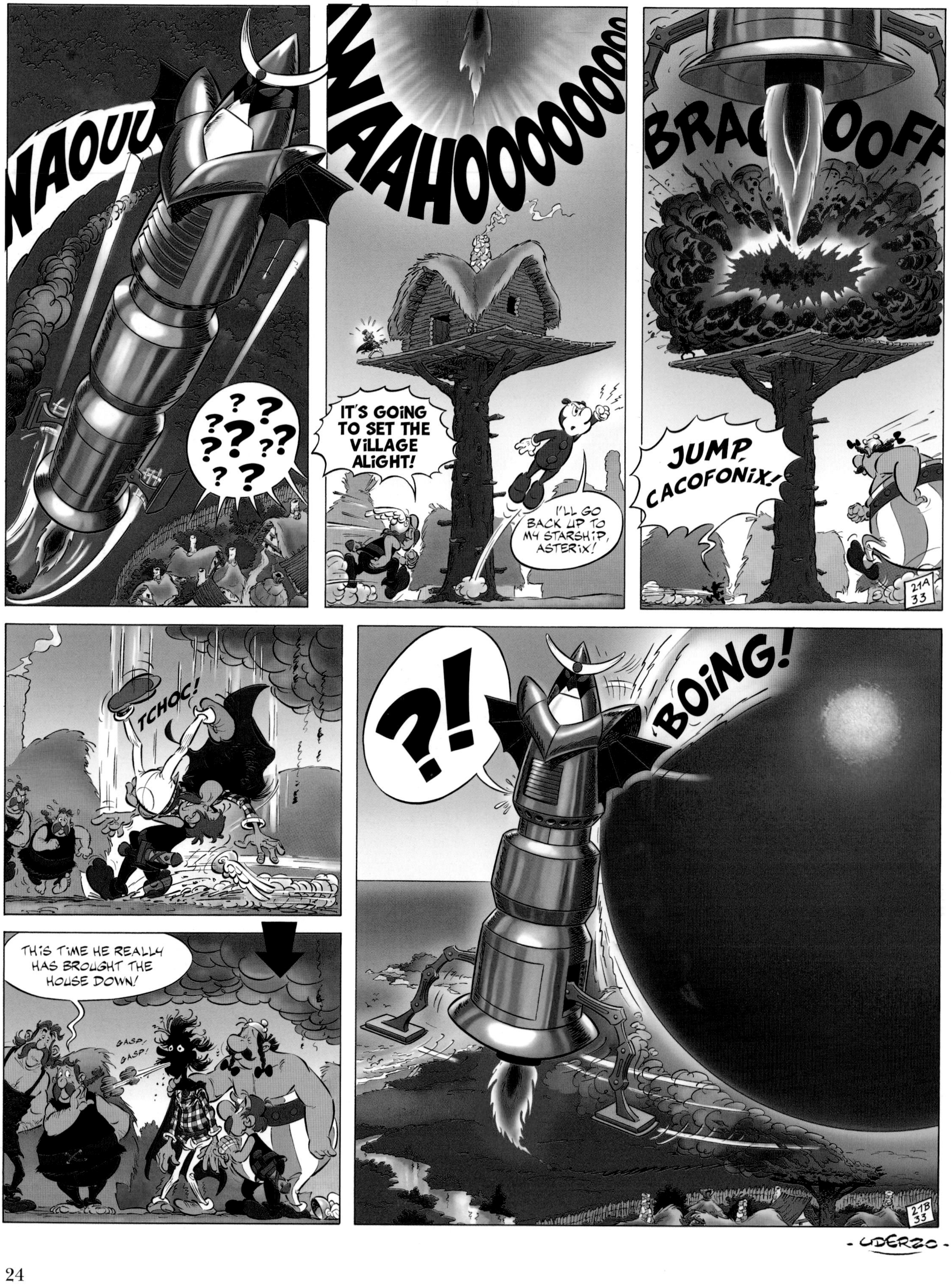

NAOUU
WAAHOOOOOOOO
BRAC
OOFF
IT'S GOING TO SET THE VILLAGE ALIGHT!
I'LL GO BACK UP TO MY STARSHIP, ASTERIX!
JUMP, CACOFONIX!
21A 33
TCHOC!
?!
BOING!
THIS TIME HE REALLY HAS BROUGHT THE HOUSE DOWN!
GASP, GASP!
21B 33
UDERZO

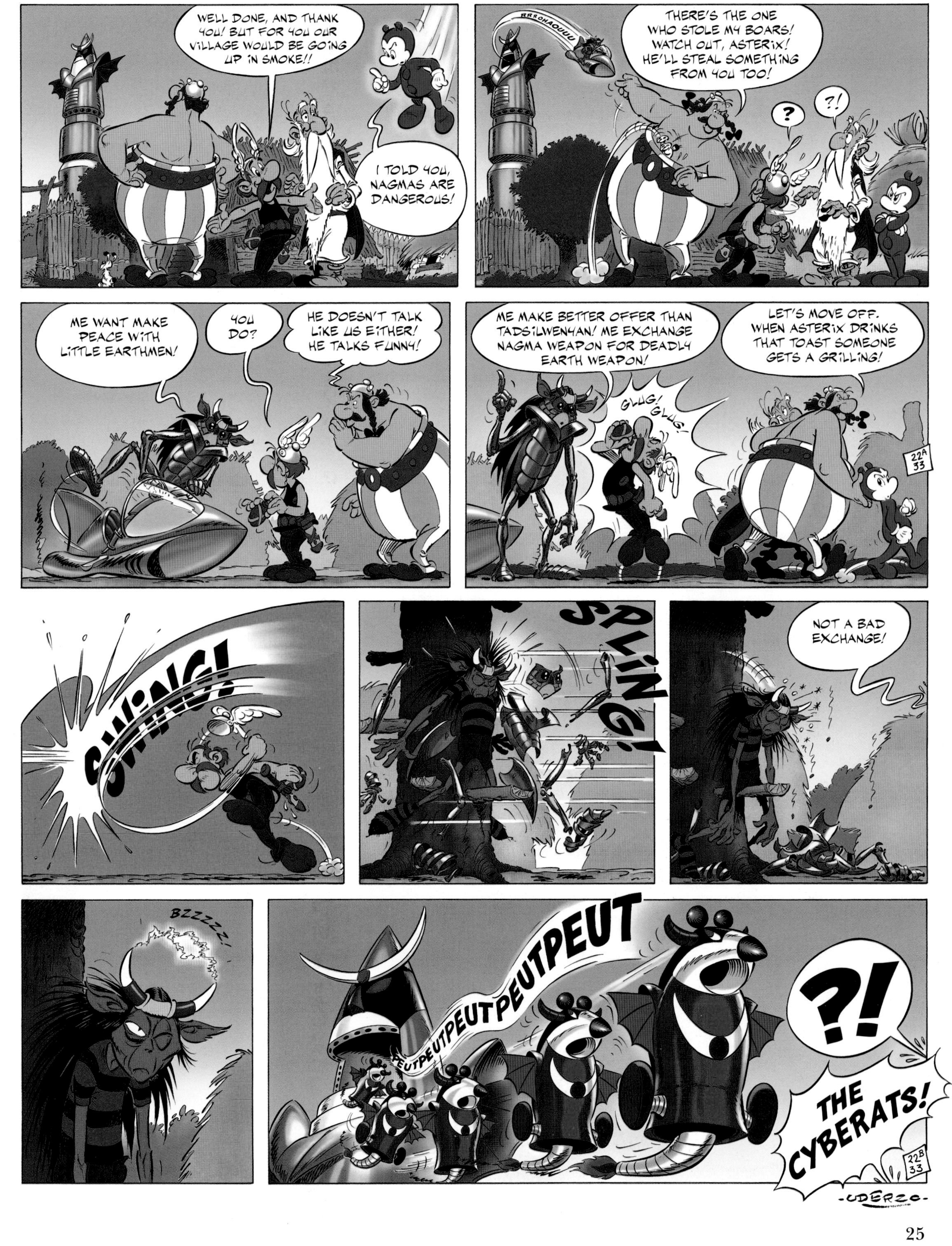
WELL DONE, AND THANK YOU! BUT FOR YOU OUR VILLAGE WOULD BE GOING UP IN SMOKE!!
I TOLD YOU, NAGMAS ARE DANGEROUS!
THERE'S THE ONE WHO STOLE MY BOARS! WATCH OUT, ASTERIX! HE'LL STEAL SOMETHING FROM YOU TOO!
?
?!
ME WANT MAKE PEACE WITH LITTLE EARTHMEN!
YOU DO?
HE DOESN'T TALK LIKE US EITHER! HE TALKS FUNNY!
ME MAKE BETTER OFFER THAN TADSILWENYAN! ME EXCHANGE NAGMA WEAPON FOR DEADLY EARTH WEAPON!
GLUG! GLUG!
LET'S MOVE OFF. WHEN ASTERIX DRINKS THAT TOAST SOMEONE GETS A GRILLING!
SWING!
SPLING!
NOT A BAD EXCHANGE!
BZZZZZZ!
PEUTPEUTPEUTPEUTPEUTPEUT
?!
THE CYBERATS!
-UDERZO-

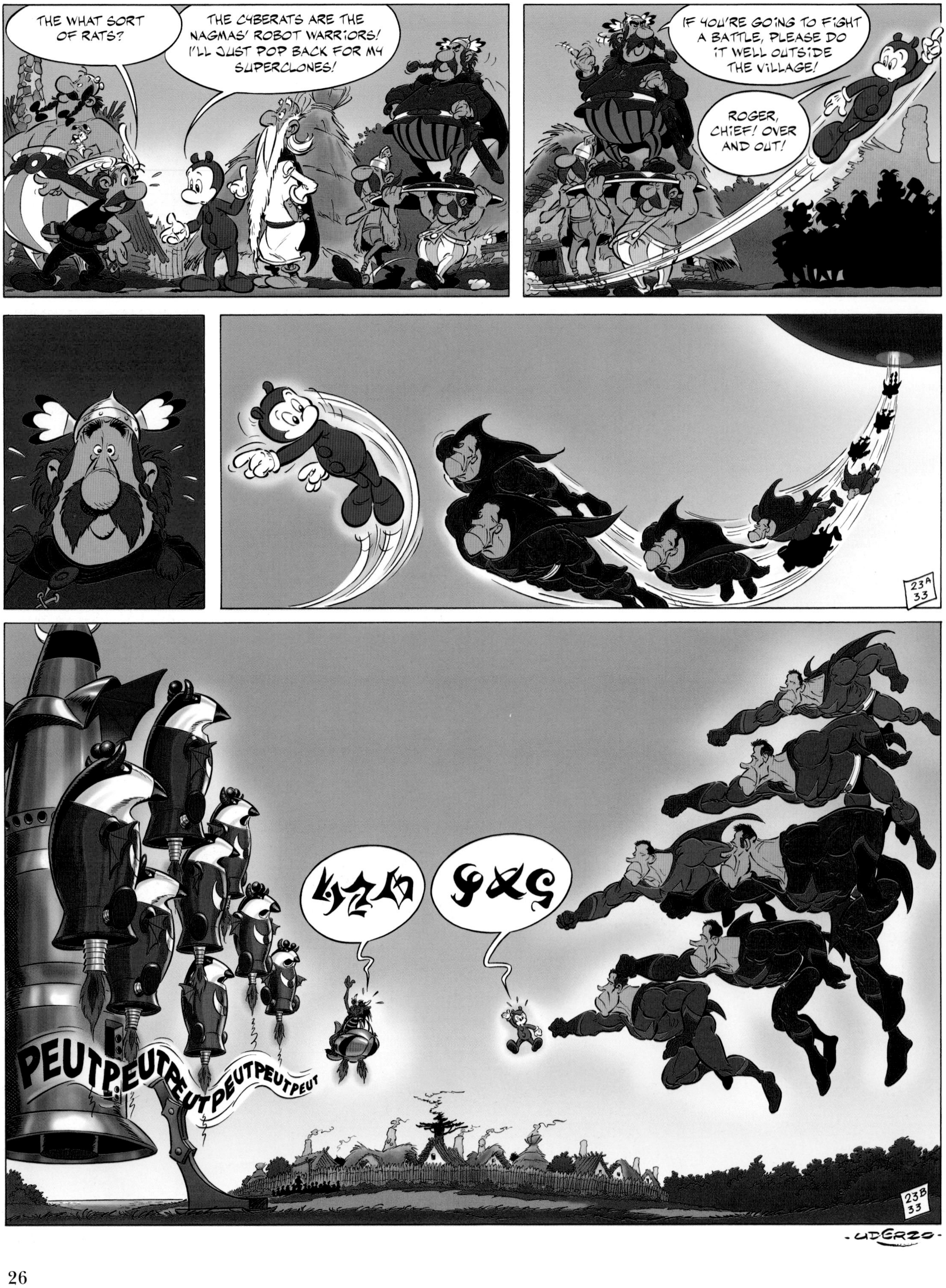
THE WHAT SORT OF RATS?
THE CYBERATS ARE THE NAGMAS' ROBOT WARRIORS! I'LL JUST POP BACK FOR MY SUPERCLONES!
IF YOU'RE GOING TO FIGHT A BATTLE, PLEASE DO IT WELL OUTSIDE THE VILLAGE!
ROGER, CHIEF! OVER AND OUT!
PEUTPEUTPEUTPEUTPEUTPEUT
UDERZO

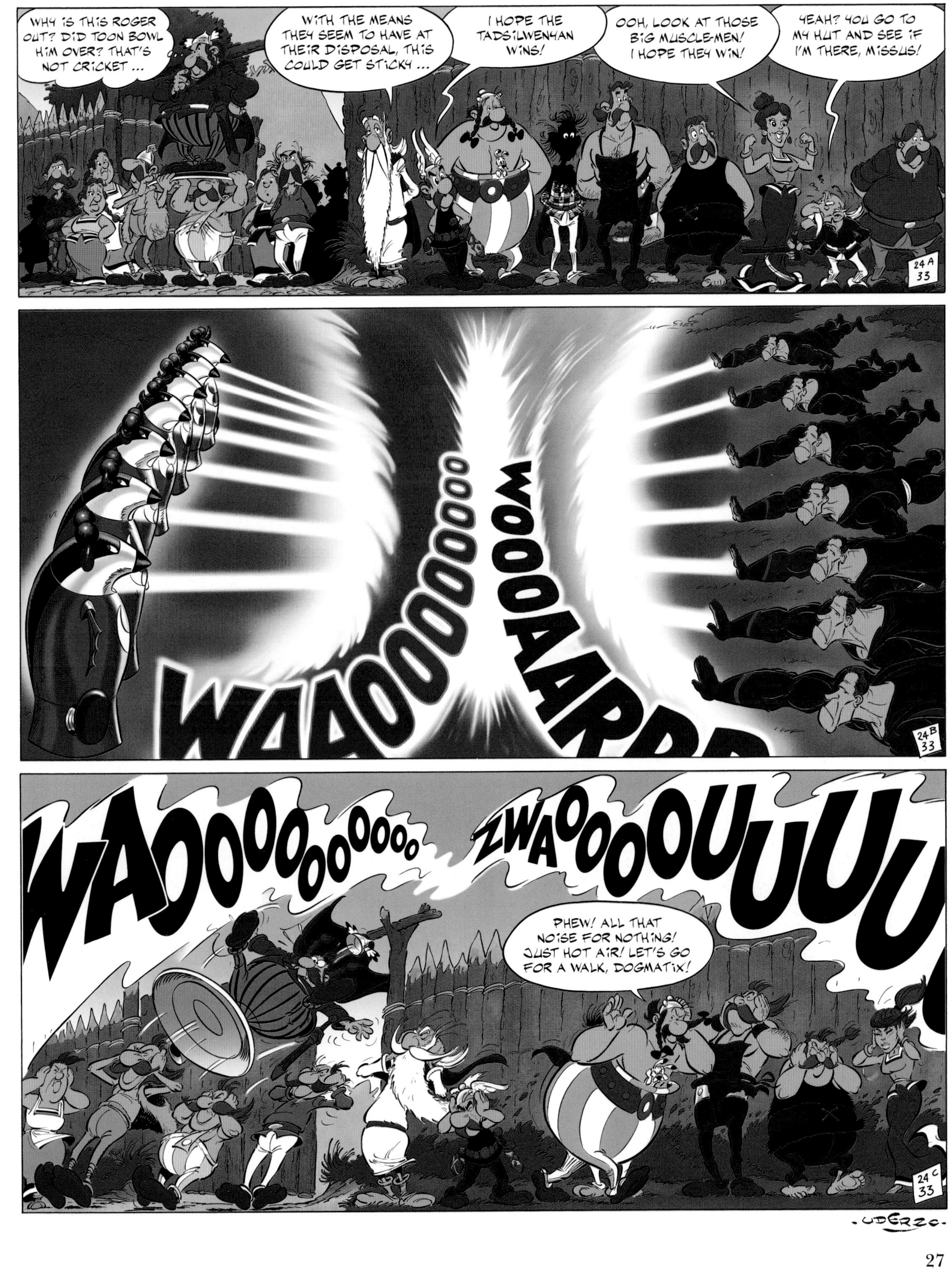
WHY IS THIS ROGER OUT? DID TOON BOWL HIM OVER? THAT'S NOT CRICKET ...
WITH THE MEANS THEY SEEM TO HAVE AT THEIR DISPOSAL, THIS COULD GET STICKY ...
I HOPE THE TADSILWENYAN WINS!
OOH, LOOK AT THOSE BIG MUSCLE-MEN! I HOPE THEY WIN!
YEAH? YOU GO TO MY HUT AND SEE IF I'M THERE, MISSUS!
WAAOOOOOOOOOO
WOOOOAARRR
WAOOOOOOOOOO
ZWAOOOOOUUUUUU
PHEW! ALL THAT NOISE FOR NOTHING! JUST HOT AIR! LET'S GO FOR A WALK, DOGMATIX!

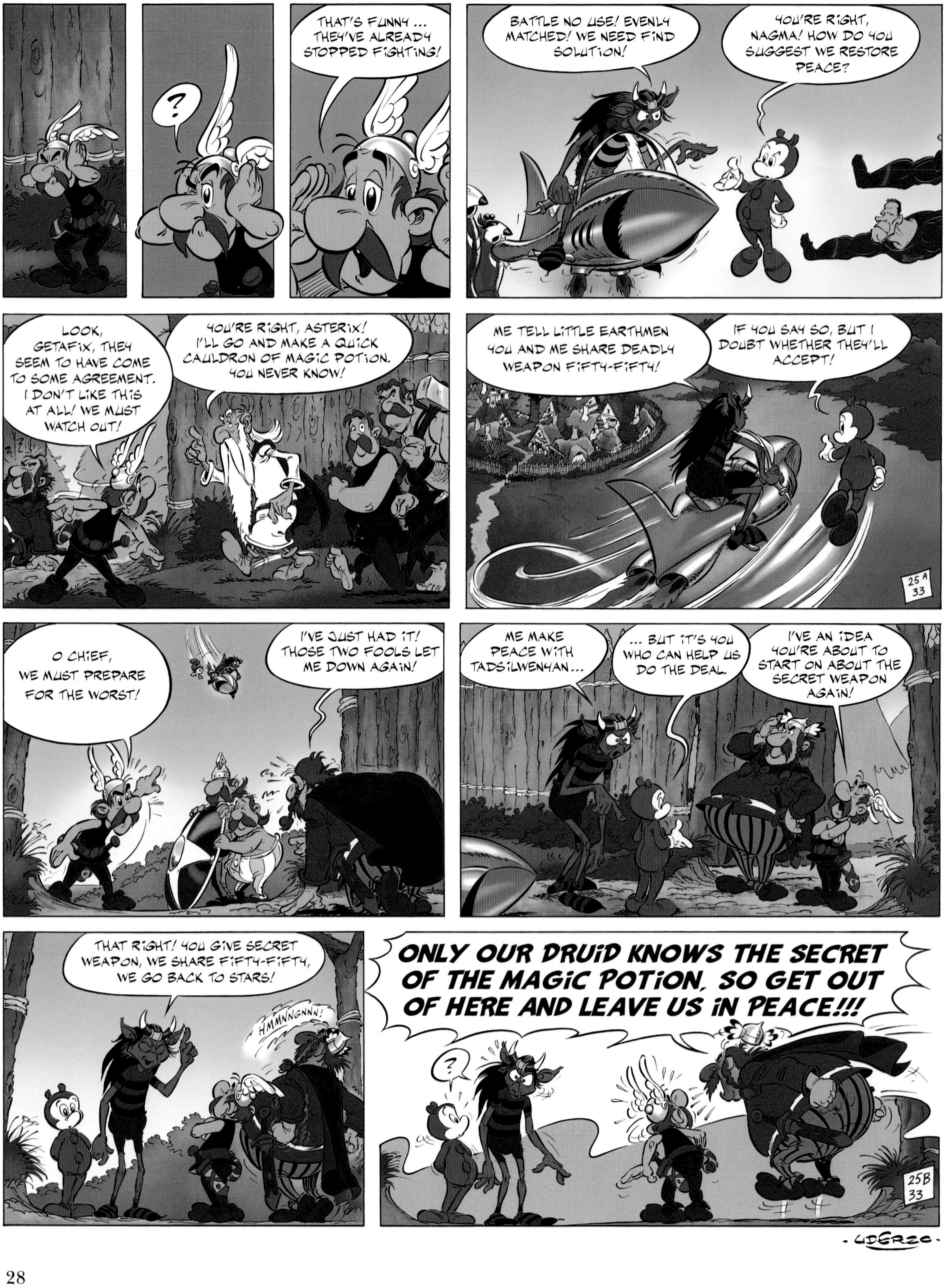
?
THAT'S FUNNY ... THEY'VE ALREADY STOPPED FIGHTING!
BATTLE NO USE! EVENLY MATCHED! WE NEED FIND SOLUTION!
YOU'RE RIGHT, NAGMA! HOW DO YOU SUGGEST WE RESTORE PEACE?
LOOK, GETAFIX, THEY SEEM TO HAVE COME TO SOME AGREEMENT. I DON'T LIKE THIS AT ALL! WE MUST WATCH OUT!
YOU'RE RIGHT, ASTERIX! I'LL GO AND MAKE A QUICK CAULDRON OF MAGIC POTION. YOU NEVER KNOW!
ME TELL LITTLE EARTHMEN YOU AND ME SHARE DEADLY WEAPON FIFTY-FIFTY!
IF YOU SAY SO, BUT I DOUBT WHETHER THEY'LL ACCEPT!
25 A 33
O CHIEF, WE MUST PREPARE FOR THE WORST!
I'VE JUST HAD IT! THOSE TWO FOOLS LET ME DOWN AGAIN!
ME MAKE PEACE WITH TADSILWENYAN...
... BUT IT'S YOU WHO CAN HELP US DO THE DEAL.
I'VE AN IDEA YOU'RE ABOUT TO START ON ABOUT THE SECRET WEAPON AGAIN!
THAT RIGHT! YOU GIVE SECRET WEAPON, WE SHARE FIFTY-FIFTY, WE GO BACK TO STARS!
HMMNNGNNN!
ONLY OUR DRUID KNOWS THE SECRET OF THE MAGIC POTION, SO GET OUT OF HERE AND LEAVE US IN PEACE!!!
?
25B 33
UDERZO

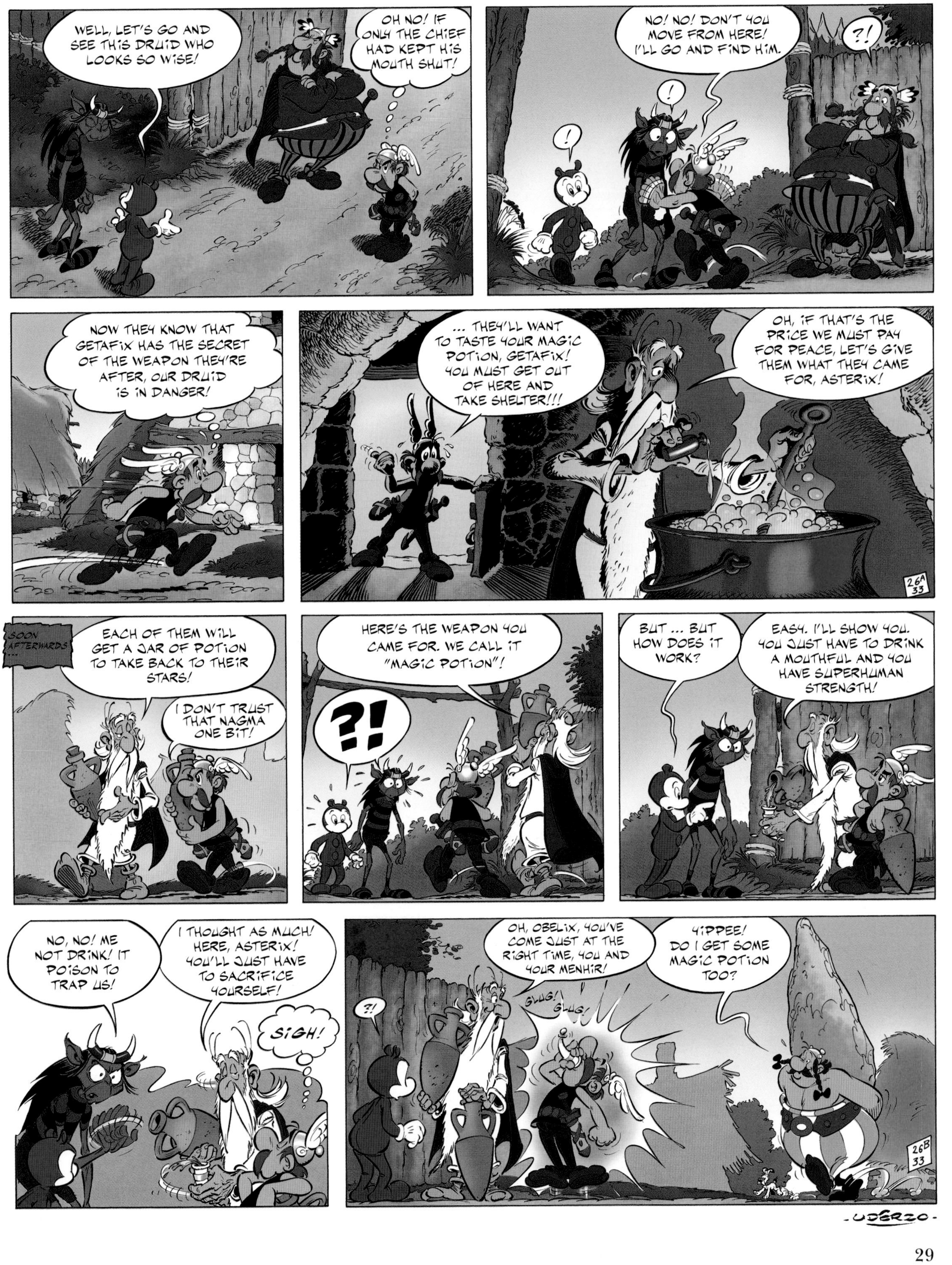

WELL, LET'S GO AND SEE THIS DRUID WHO LOOKS SO WISE!
OH NO! IF ONLY THE CHIEF HAD KEPT HIS MOUTH SHUT!
NO! NO! DON'T YOU MOVE FROM HERE! I'LL GO AND FIND HIM.
!
!
?!
NOW THEY KNOW THAT GETAFIX HAS THE SECRET OF THE WEAPON THEY'RE AFTER, OUR DRUID IS IN DANGER!
... THEY'LL WANT TO TASTE YOUR MAGIC POTION, GETAFIX! YOU MUST GET OUT OF HERE AND TAKE SHELTER!!!
OH, IF THAT'S THE PRICE WE MUST PAY FOR PEACE, LET'S GIVE THEM WHAT THEY CAME FOR, ASTERIX!
26A 33
SOON AFTERWARDS ...
EACH OF THEM WILL GET A JAR OF POTION TO TAKE BACK TO THEIR STARS!
I DON'T TRUST THAT NAGMA ONE BIT!
HERE'S THE WEAPON YOU CAME FOR. WE CALL IT "MAGIC POTION"!
?!
BUT ... BUT HOW DOES IT WORK?
EASY. I'LL SHOW YOU. YOU JUST HAVE TO DRINK A MOUTHFUL AND YOU HAVE SUPERHUMAN STRENGTH!
NO, NO! ME NOT DRINK! IT POISON TO TRAP US!
I THOUGHT AS MUCH! HERE, ASTERIX! YOU'LL JUST HAVE TO SACRIFICE YOURSELF!
SIGH!
OH, OBELIX, YOU'VE COME JUST AT THE RIGHT TIME, YOU AND YOUR MENHIR!
YIPPEE! DO I GET SOME MAGIC POTION TOO?
?!
GLUG! GLUG!
26B 33
UDERZO

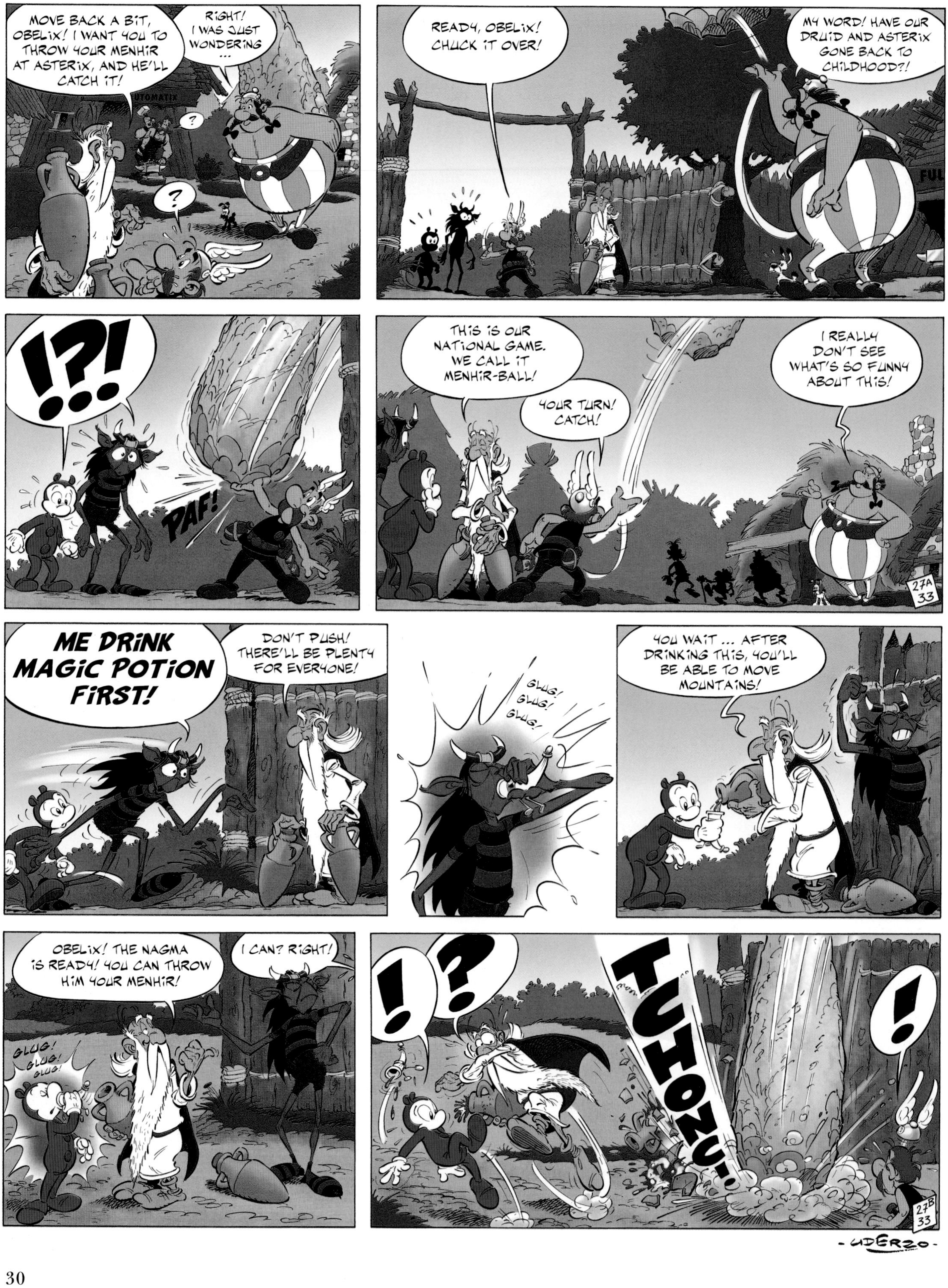
MOVE BACK A BIT, OBELIX! I WANT YOU TO THROW YOUR MENHIR AT ASTERIX, AND HE'LL CATCH IT!
RIGHT! I WAS JUST WONDERING ...
?
?
READY, OBELIX! CHUCK IT OVER!
MY WORD! HAVE OUR DRUID AND ASTERIX GONE BACK TO CHILDHOOD?!
!?!...
PAF!
THIS IS OUR NATIONAL GAME. WE CALL IT MENHIR-BALL!
YOUR TURN! CATCH!
I REALLY DON'T SEE WHAT'S SO FUNNY ABOUT THIS!
ME DRINK MAGIC POTION FIRST!
DON'T PUSH! THERE'LL BE PLENTY FOR EVERYONE!
GLUG! GLUG! GLUG!
YOU WAIT ... AFTER DRINKING THIS, YOU'LL BE ABLE TO MOVE MOUNTAINS!
OBELIX! THE NAGMA IS READY! YOU CAN THROW HIM YOUR MENHIR!
I CAN? RIGHT!
GLUG! GLUG! GLUG!
!
?
TCHONC!
!
UDERZO

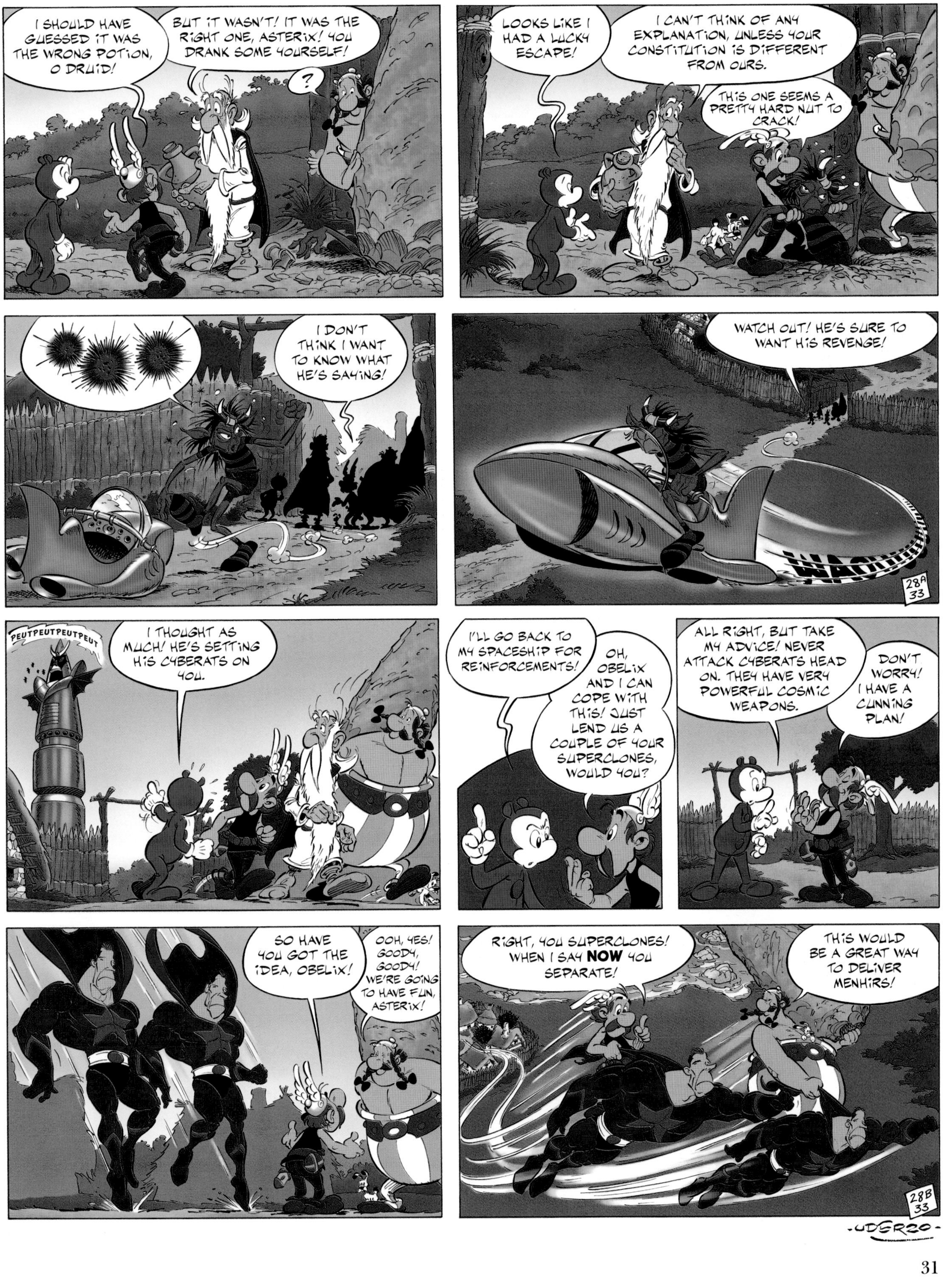
I SHOULD HAVE GUESSED IT WAS THE WRONG POTION, O DRUID!
BUT IT WASN'T! IT WAS THE RIGHT ONE, ASTERIX! YOU DRANK SOME YOURSELF!
?
LOOKS LIKE I HAD A LUCKY ESCAPE!
I CAN'T THINK OF ANY EXPLANATION, UNLESS YOUR CONSTITUTION IS DIFFERENT FROM OURS.
THIS ONE SEEMS A PRETTY HARD NUT TO CRACK!
I DON'T THINK I WANT TO KNOW WHAT HE'S SAYING!
WATCH OUT! HE'S SURE TO WANT HIS REVENGE!
28A 33
PEUTPEUTPEUTPEUT
I THOUGHT AS MUCH! HE'S SETTING HIS CYBERATS ON YOU.
I'LL GO BACK TO MY SPACESHIP FOR REINFORCEMENTS!
OH, OBELIX AND I CAN COPE WITH THIS! JUST LEND US A COUPLE OF YOUR SUPERCLONES, WOULD YOU?
ALL RIGHT, BUT TAKE MY ADVICE! NEVER ATTACK CYBERATS HEAD ON. THEY HAVE VERY POWERFUL COSMIC WEAPONS.
DON'T WORRY! I HAVE A CUNNING PLAN!
SO HAVE YOU GOT THE IDEA, OBELIX!
OOH, YES! GOODY, GOODY! WE'RE GOING TO HAVE FUN, ASTERIX!
RIGHT, YOU SUPERCLONES! WHEN I SAY **NOW** YOU SEPARATE!
THIS WOULD BE A GREAT WAY TO DELIVER MENHIRS!
28B 33
UDERZO

WATCH OUT!
PEUTPEUTPEUT
NOW!
PEUTPEUTPEUTPEUT
PEUTPEUTPEUTPEUTPEUTPEUTPEUT
OVER TO YOU, OBELIX!
TCHRAC!
IT'S MUCH MORE FUN LIKE THIS!
GOOD SHOT, OBELIX! OCULUS TAURI!*

* BULL'S-EYE IN GALLO-ROMAN TIMES.

- UDERZO -

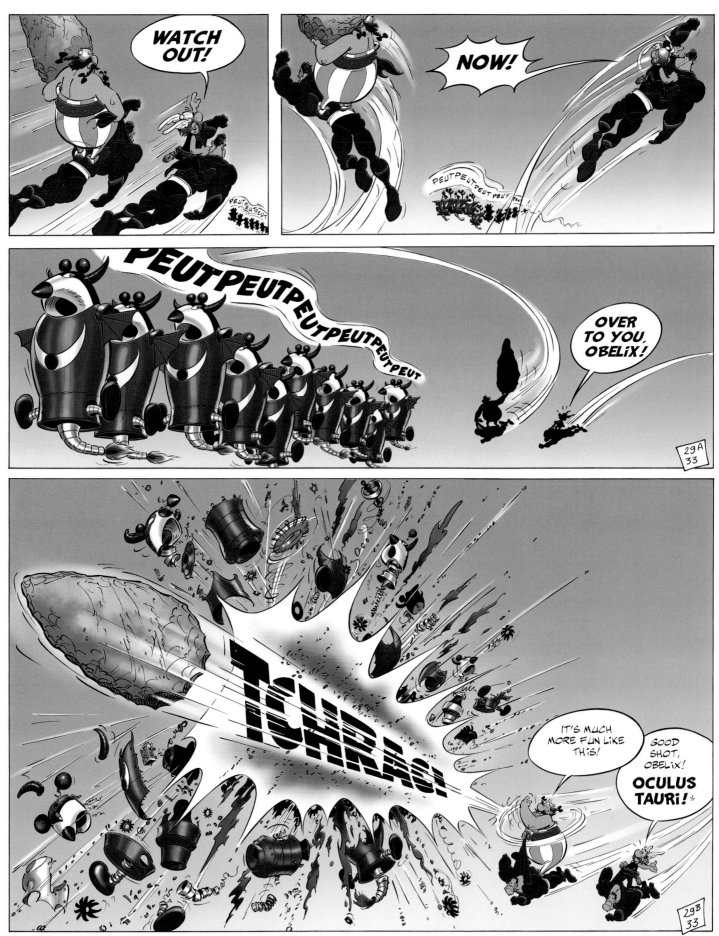

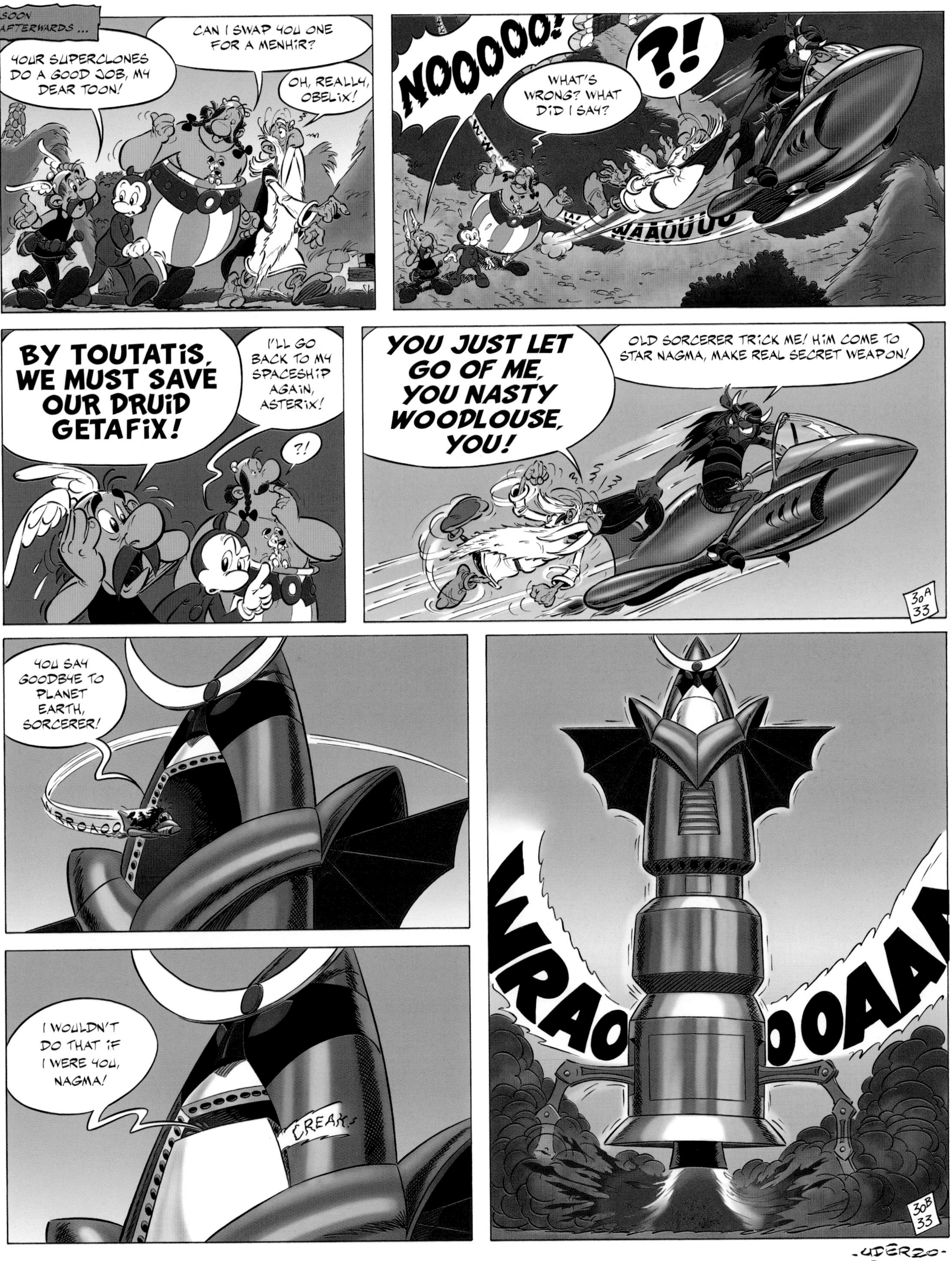
SOON AFTERWARDS ...
YOUR SUPERCLONES DO A GOOD JOB, MY DEAR TOON!
CAN I SWAP YOU ONE FOR A MENHIR?
OH, REALLY, OBELIX!
NOOOOO!
WHAT'S WRONG? WHAT DID I SAY?
?!
WAAOUUU
BY TOUTATIS, WE MUST SAVE OUR DRUID GETAFIX!
I'LL GO BACK TO MY SPACESHIP AGAIN, ASTERIX!
?!
YOU JUST LET GO OF ME, YOU NASTY WOODLOUSE, YOU!
OLD SORCERER TRICK ME! HIM COME TO STAR NAGMA, MAKE REAL SECRET WEAPON!
YOU SAY GOODBYE TO PLANET EARTH, SORCERER!
WRROAOO
I WOULDN'T DO THAT IF I WERE YOU, NAGMA!
CREAK
WRAOOOAAA
UDERZO

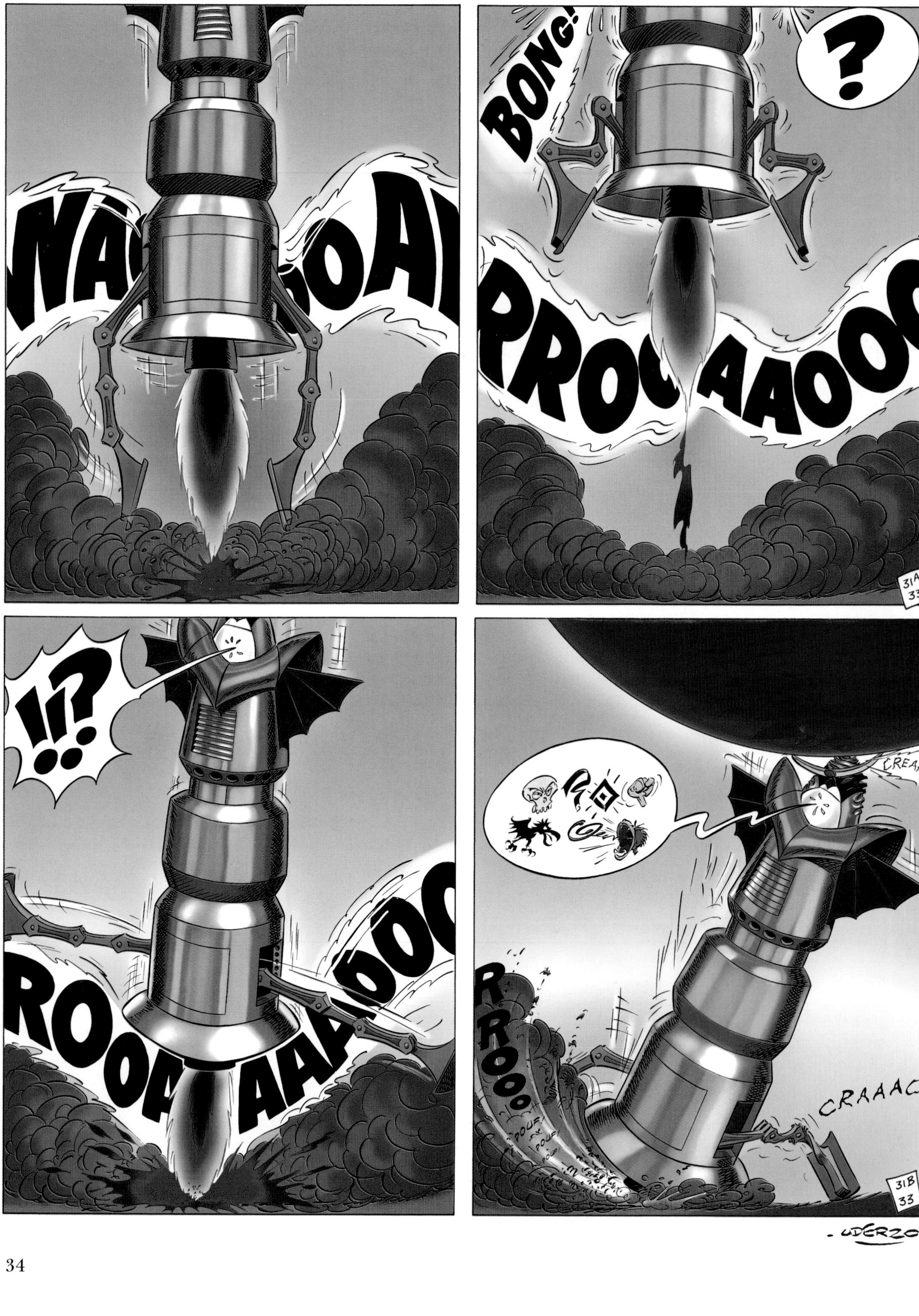
WAÂ
OOAH
BONG!
?
PROO
AAOOO
31A
33
!!?
ROOF
AAAOOO
CREAK
RROOO
POUF
CRAAAC
31B
33
UDERZO

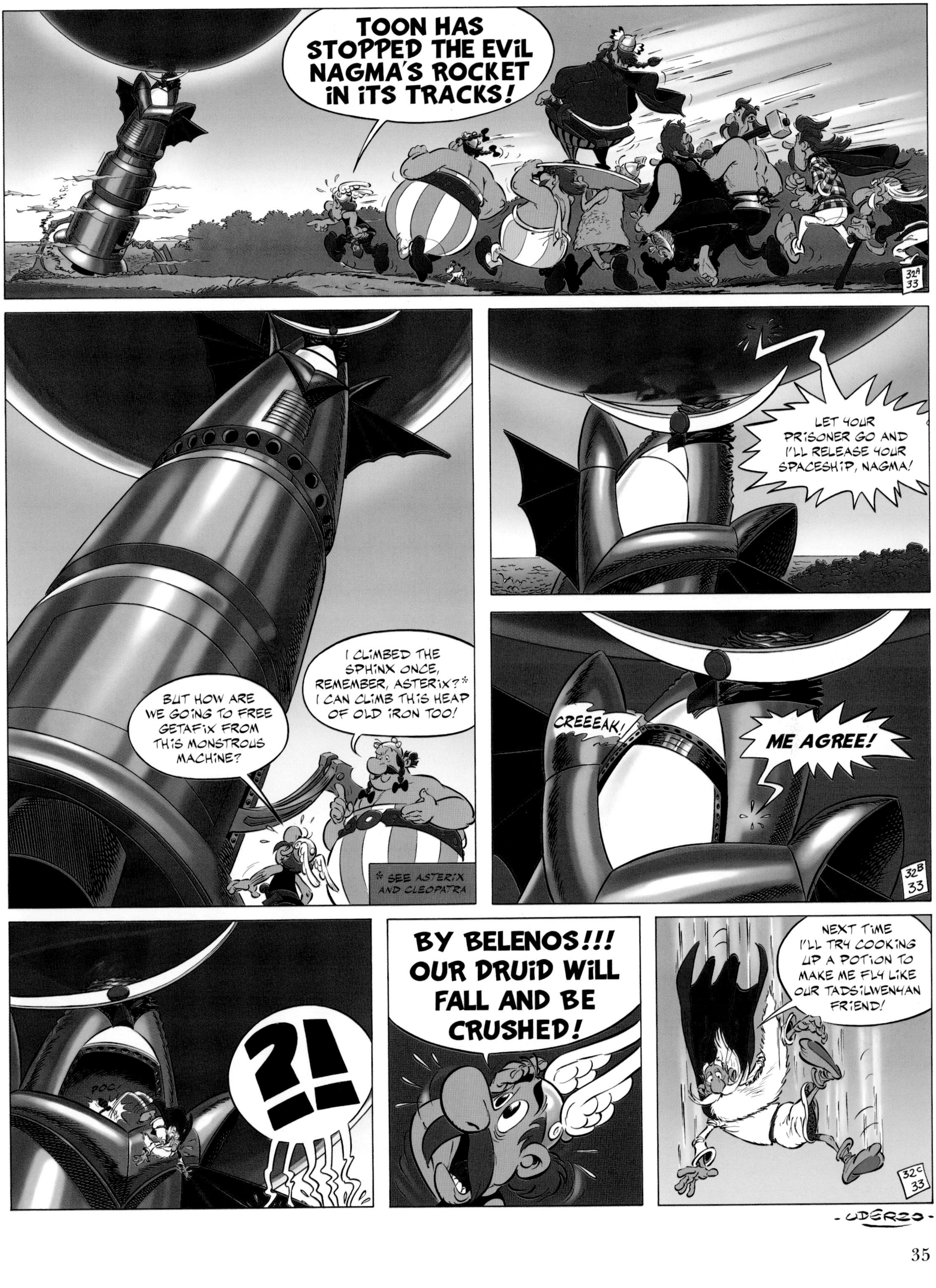
TOON HAS STOPPED THE EVIL NAGMA'S ROCKET IN ITS TRACKS!
BUT HOW ARE WE GOING TO FREE GETAFIX FROM THIS MONSTROUS MACHINE?
I CLIMBED THE SPHINX ONCE, REMEMBER, ASTERIX?* I CAN CLIMB THIS HEAP OF OLD IRON TOO!
* SEE ASTERIX AND CLEOPATRA
LET YOUR PRISONER GO AND I'LL RELEASE YOUR SPACESHIP, NAGMA!
CREEEAK!
ME AGREE!
POC
?!
BY BELENOS!!! OUR DRUID WILL FALL AND BE CRUSHED!
NEXT TIME I'LL TRY COOKING UP A POTION TO MAKE ME FLY LIKE OUR TADSILWENYAN FRIEND!
UDERZO

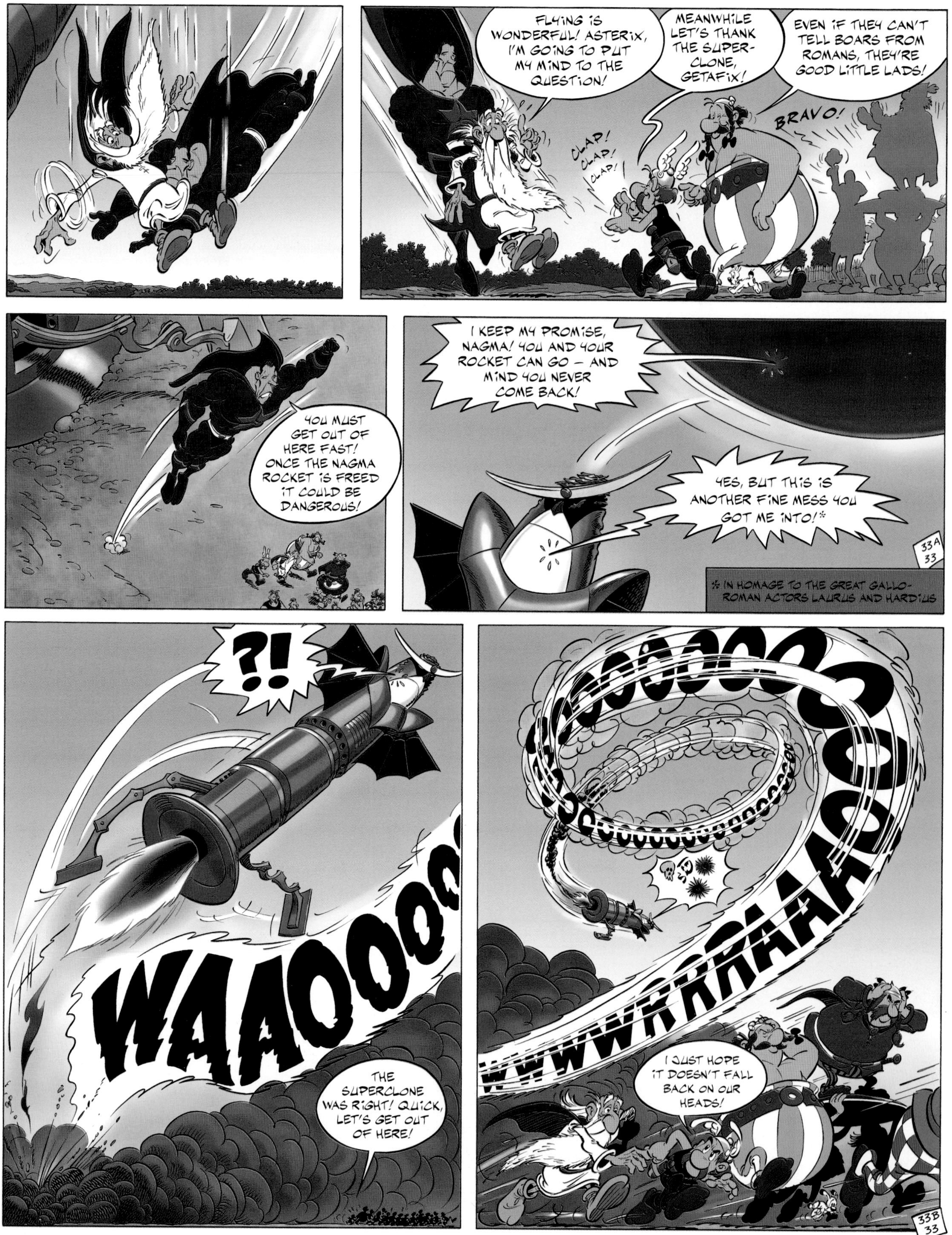
FLYING IS WONDERFUL! ASTERIX, I'M GOING TO PUT MY MIND TO THE QUESTION!
MEANWHILE LET'S THANK THE SUPER-CLONE, GETAFIX!
EVEN IF THEY CAN'T TELL BOARS FROM ROMANS, THEY'RE GOOD LITTLE LADS!
CLAP! CLAP! CLAP!
BRAVO!
YOU MUST GET OUT OF HERE FAST! ONCE THE NAGMA ROCKET IS FREED IT COULD BE DANGEROUS!
I KEEP MY PROMISE, NAGMA! YOU AND YOUR ROCKET CAN GO – AND MIND YOU NEVER COME BACK!
YES, BUT THIS IS ANOTHER FINE MESS YOU GOT ME INTO!*
33A 33
* IN HOMAGE TO THE GREAT GALLO-ROMAN ACTORS LAURUS AND HARDIUS
?!
WAAOOOO
THE SUPERCLONE WAS RIGHT! QUICK, LET'S GET OUT OF HERE!
I JUST HOPE IT DOESN'T FALL BACK ON OUR HEADS!
33B 33
UDERZO

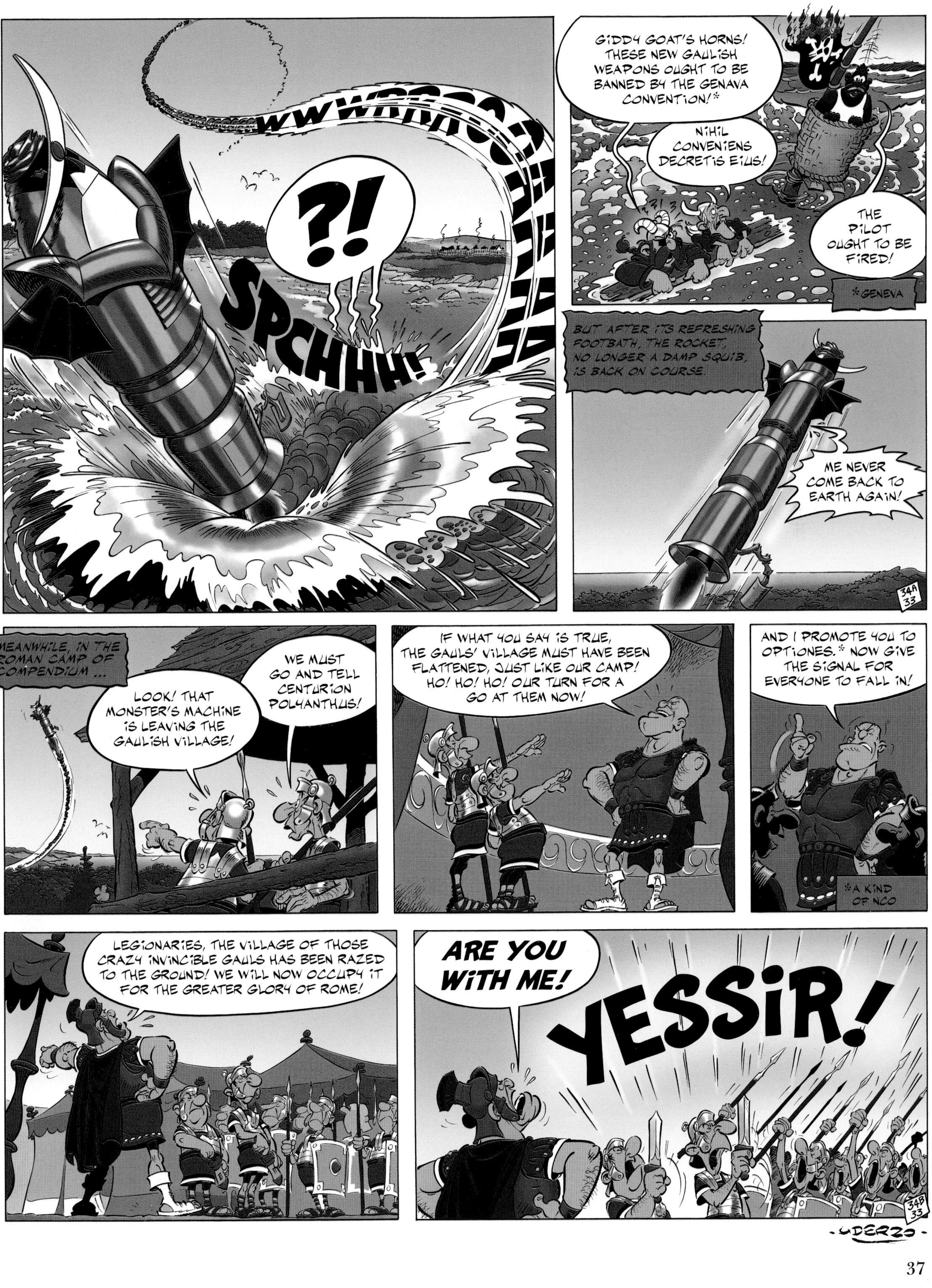
?!
SPCHHH!
GIDDY GOAT'S HORNS! THESE NEW GAULISH WEAPONS OUGHT TO BE BANNED BY THE GENAVA CONVENTION!*
NIHIL CONVENIENS DECRETIS EIUS!
THE PILOT OUGHT TO BE FIRED!
*GENEVA
BUT AFTER ITS REFRESHING FOOTBATH, THE ROCKET, NO LONGER A DAMP SQUIB, IS BACK ON COURSE.
ME NEVER COME BACK TO EARTH AGAIN!
MEANWHILE, IN THE ROMAN CAMP OF COMPENDIUM ...
LOOK! THAT MONSTER'S MACHINE IS LEAVING THE GAULISH VILLAGE!
WE MUST GO AND TELL CENTURION POLYANTHUS!
IF WHAT YOU SAY IS TRUE, THE GAULS' VILLAGE MUST HAVE BEEN FLATTENED, JUST LIKE OUR CAMP! HO! HO! HO! OUR TURN FOR A GO AT THEM NOW!
AND I PROMOTE YOU TO OPTIONES.* NOW GIVE THE SIGNAL FOR EVERYONE TO FALL IN!
*A KIND OF NCO
LEGIONARIES, THE VILLAGE OF THOSE CRAZY INVINCIBLE GAULS HAS BEEN RAZED TO THE GROUND! WE WILL NOW OCCUPY IT FOR THE GREATER GLORY OF ROME!
ARE YOU WITH ME!
YESSIR!
-UDERZO-

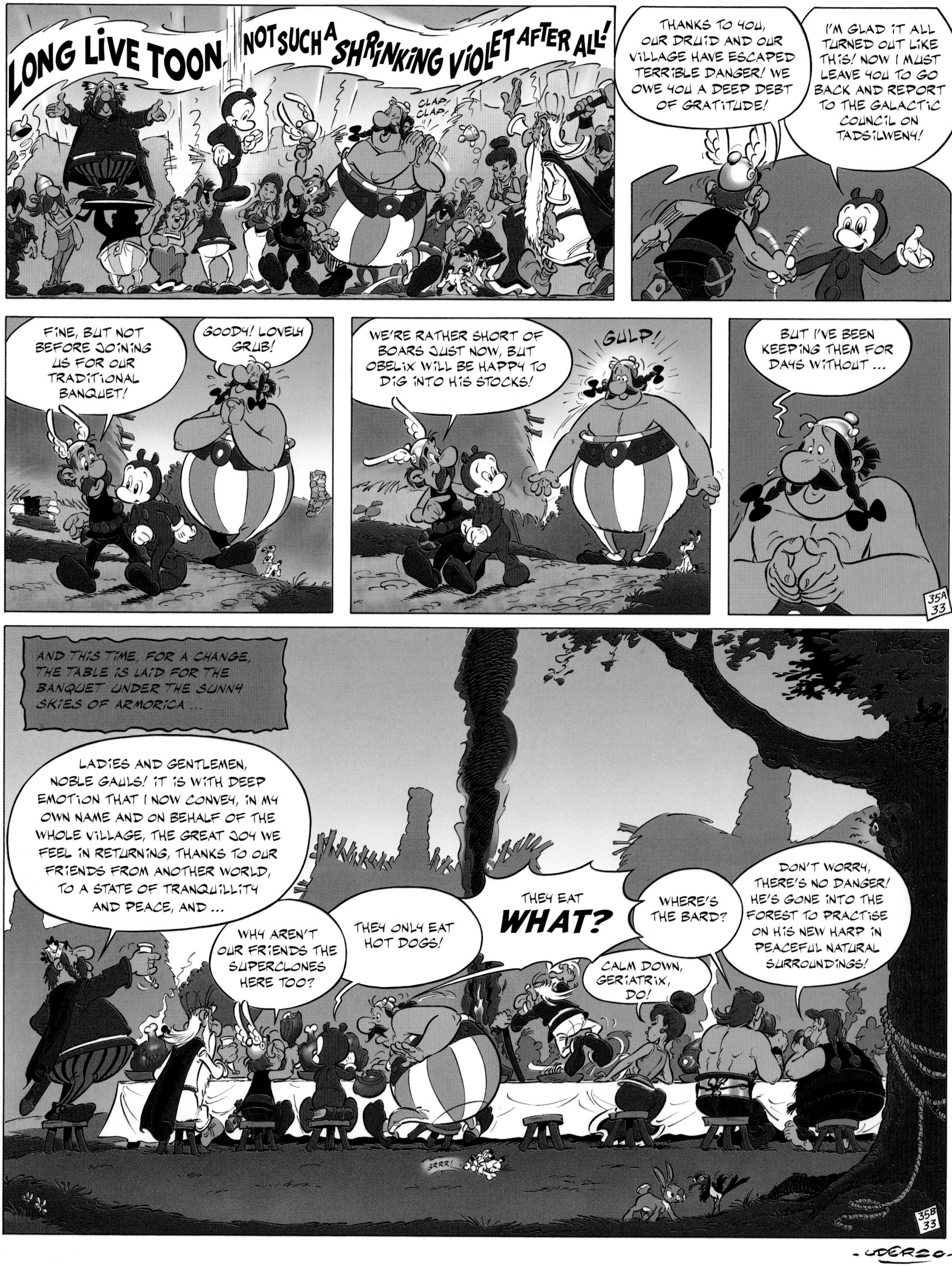
LONG LIVE TOON, NOT SUCH A SHRINKING VIOLET AFTER ALL!
CLAP! CLAP!
THANKS TO YOU, OUR DRUID AND OUR VILLAGE HAVE ESCAPED TERRIBLE DANGER! WE OWE YOU A DEEP DEBT OF GRATITUDE!
I'M GLAD IT ALL TURNED OUT LIKE THIS! NOW I MUST LEAVE YOU TO GO BACK AND REPORT TO THE GALACTIC COUNCIL ON TADSILWENY!
FINE, BUT NOT BEFORE JOINING US FOR OUR TRADITIONAL BANQUET!
GOODY! LOVELY GRUB!
WE'RE RATHER SHORT OF BOARS JUST NOW, BUT OBELIX WILL BE HAPPY TO DIG INTO HIS STOCKS!
GULP!
BUT I'VE BEEN KEEPING THEM FOR DAYS WITHOUT ...
35A 33
AND THIS TIME, FOR A CHANGE, THE TABLE IS LAID FOR THE BANQUET UNDER THE SUNNY SKIES OF ARMORICA ...
LADIES AND GENTLEMEN, NOBLE GAULS! IT IS WITH DEEP EMOTION THAT I NOW CONVEY, IN MY OWN NAME AND ON BEHALF OF THE WHOLE VILLAGE, THE GREAT JOY WE FEEL IN RETURNING, THANKS TO OUR FRIENDS FROM ANOTHER WORLD, TO A STATE OF TRANQUILLITY AND PEACE, AND ...
WHY AREN'T OUR FRIENDS THE SUPERCLONES HERE TOO?
THEY ONLY EAT HOT DOGS!
THEY EAT WHAT?
WHERE'S THE BARD?
CALM DOWN, GERIATRIX, DO!
DON'T WORRY, THERE'S NO DANGER! HE'S GONE INTO THE FOREST TO PRACTISE ON HIS NEW HARP IN PEACEFUL NATURAL SURROUNDINGS!
GRRR!
35B 33
UDERZO

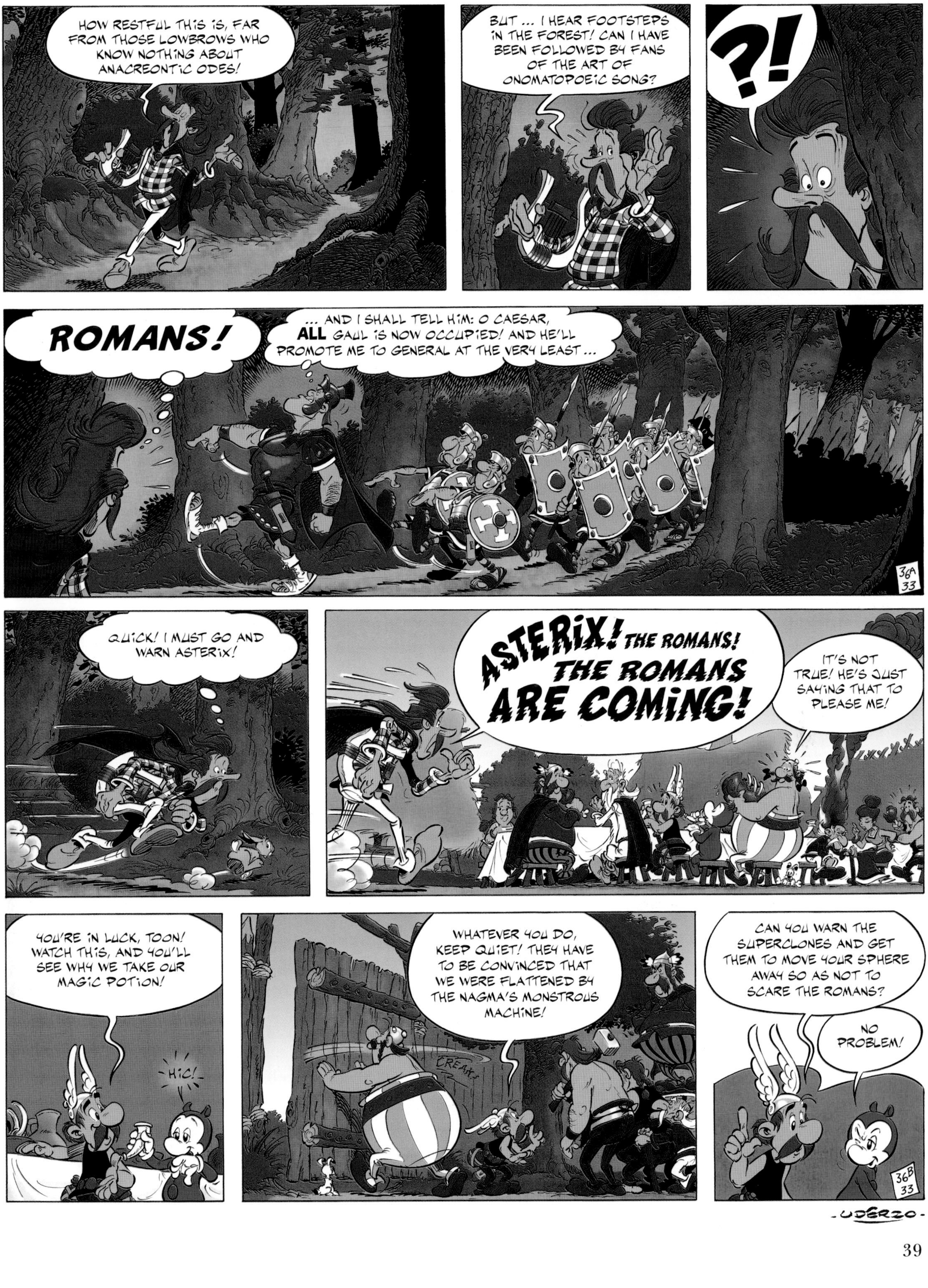
HOW RESTFUL THIS IS, FAR FROM THOSE LOWBROWS WHO KNOW NOTHING ABOUT ANACREONTIC ODES!
BUT ... I HEAR FOOTSTEPS IN THE FOREST! CAN I HAVE BEEN FOLLOWED BY FANS OF THE ART OF ONOMATOPOEIC SONG?
?!
ROMANS!
... AND I SHALL TELL HIM: O CAESAR, ALL GAUL IS NOW OCCUPIED! AND HE'LL PROMOTE ME TO GENERAL AT THE VERY LEAST ...
QUICK! I MUST GO AND WARN ASTERIX!
ASTERIX! THE ROMANS! THE ROMANS ARE COMING!
IT'S NOT TRUE! HE'S JUST SAYING THAT TO PLEASE ME!
YOU'RE IN LUCK, TOON! WATCH THIS, AND YOU'LL SEE WHY WE TAKE OUR MAGIC POTION!
HIC!
WHATEVER YOU DO, KEEP QUIET! THEY HAVE TO BE CONVINCED THAT WE WERE FLATTENED BY THE NAGMA'S MONSTROUS MACHINE!
CREAK
CAN YOU WARN THE SUPERCLONES AND GET THEM TO MOVE YOUR SPHERE AWAY SO AS NOT TO SCARE THE ROMANS?
NO PROBLEM!
UDERZO

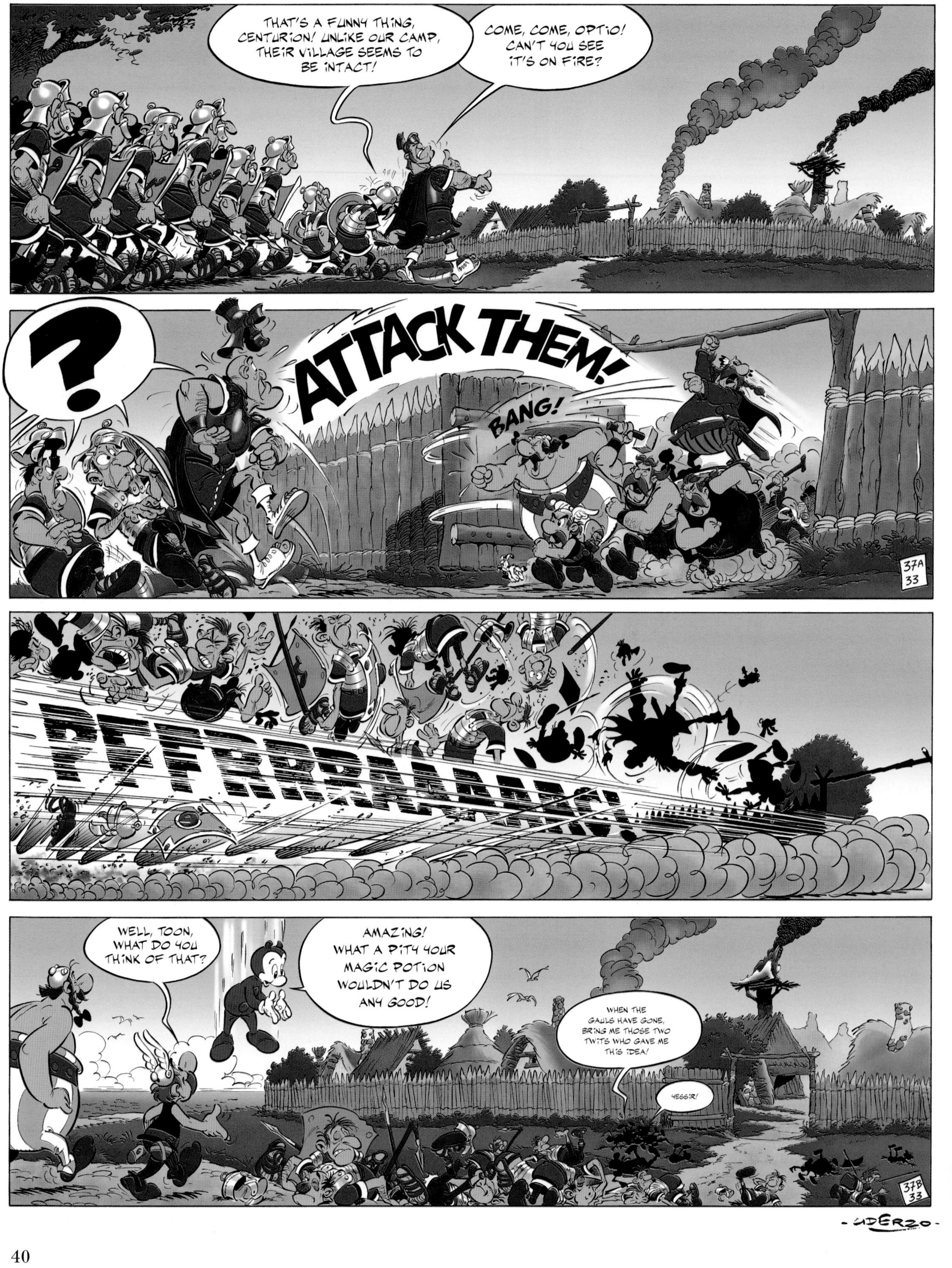
THAT'S A FUNNY THING, CENTURION! UNLIKE OUR CAMP, THEIR VILLAGE SEEMS TO BE INTACT!
COME, COME, OPTIO! CAN'T YOU SEE IT'S ON FIRE?
?
ATTACK THEM!
BANG!
WELL, TOON, WHAT DO YOU THINK OF THAT?
AMAZING! WHAT A PITY YOUR MAGIC POTION WOULDN'T DO US ANY GOOD!
WHEN THE GAULS HAVE GONE, BRING ME THOSE TWO TWITS WHO GAVE ME THIS IDEA!
YESSIR!

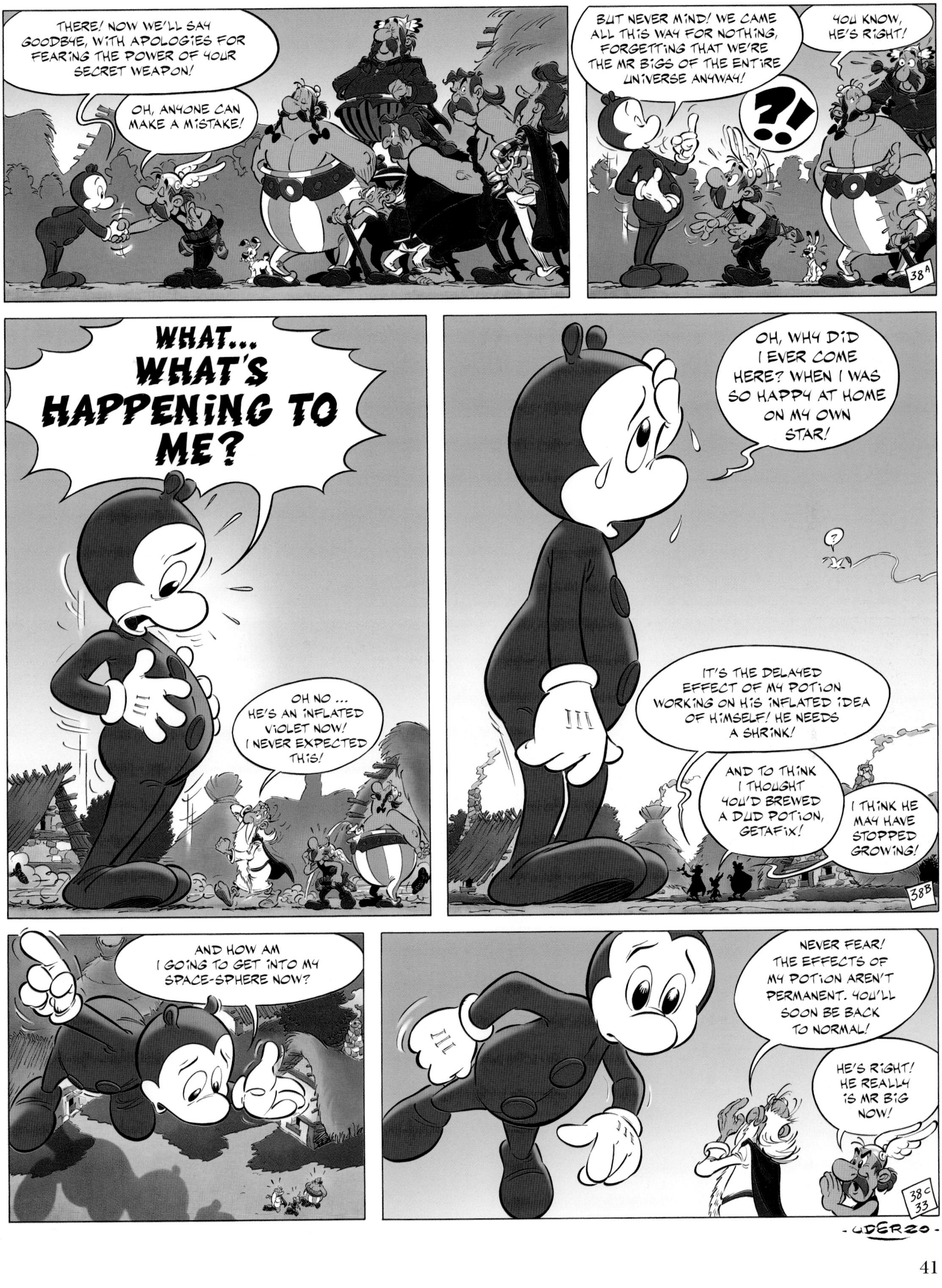
THERE! NOW WE'LL SAY GOODBYE, WITH APOLOGIES FOR FEARING THE POWER OF YOUR SECRET WEAPON!
OH, ANYONE CAN MAKE A MISTAKE!
BUT NEVER MIND! WE CAME ALL THIS WAY FOR NOTHING, FORGETTING THAT WE'RE THE MR BIGS OF THE ENTIRE UNIVERSE ANYWAY!
?!
YOU KNOW, HE'S RIGHT!
38A
WHAT... WHAT'S HAPPENING TO ME?
OH NO ... HE'S AN INFLATED VIOLET NOW! I NEVER EXPECTED THIS!
OH, WHY DID I EVER COME HERE? WHEN I WAS SO HAPPY AT HOME ON MY OWN STAR!
?
IT'S THE DELAYED EFFECT OF MY POTION WORKING ON HIS INFLATED IDEA OF HIMSELF! HE NEEDS A SHRINK!
AND TO THINK I THOUGHT YOU'D BREWED A DUD POTION, GETAFIX!
I THINK HE MAY HAVE STOPPED GROWING!
38B
AND HOW AM I GOING TO GET INTO MY SPACE-SPHERE NOW?
NEVER FEAR! THE EFFECTS OF MY POTION AREN'T PERMANENT. YOU'LL SOON BE BACK TO NORMAL!
HE'S RIGHT! HE REALLY IS MR BIG NOW!
38C 33
UDERZO

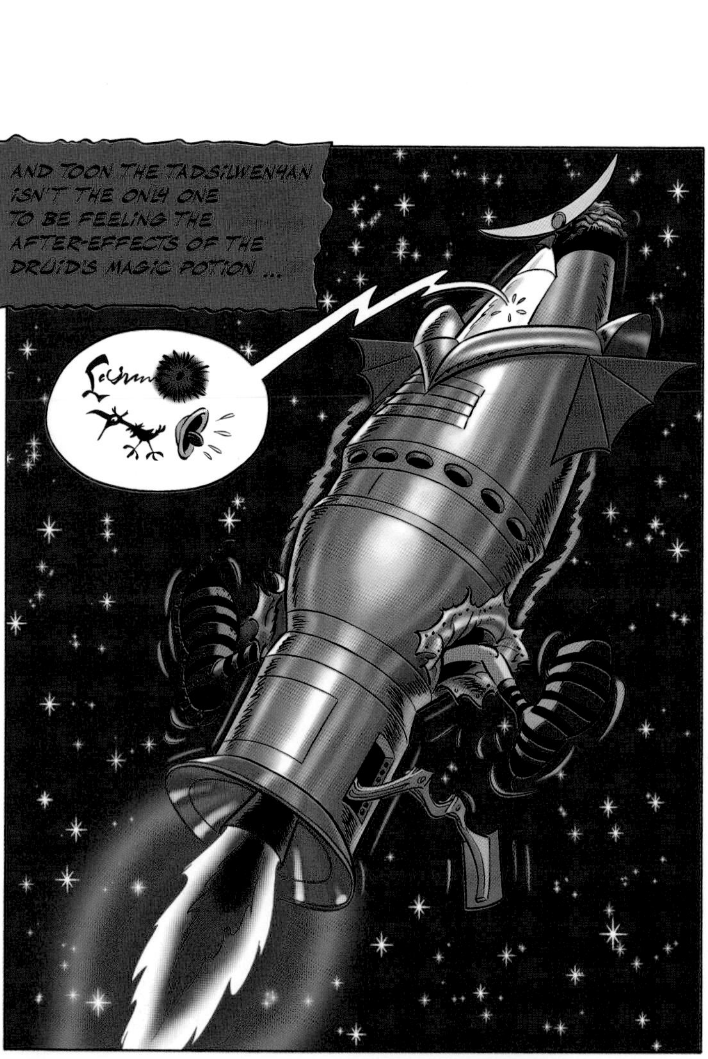
AND TOON THE TADSILWENYAN ISN'T THE ONLY ONE TO BE FEELING THE AFTER-EFFECTS OF THE DRUID'S MAGIC POTION ...

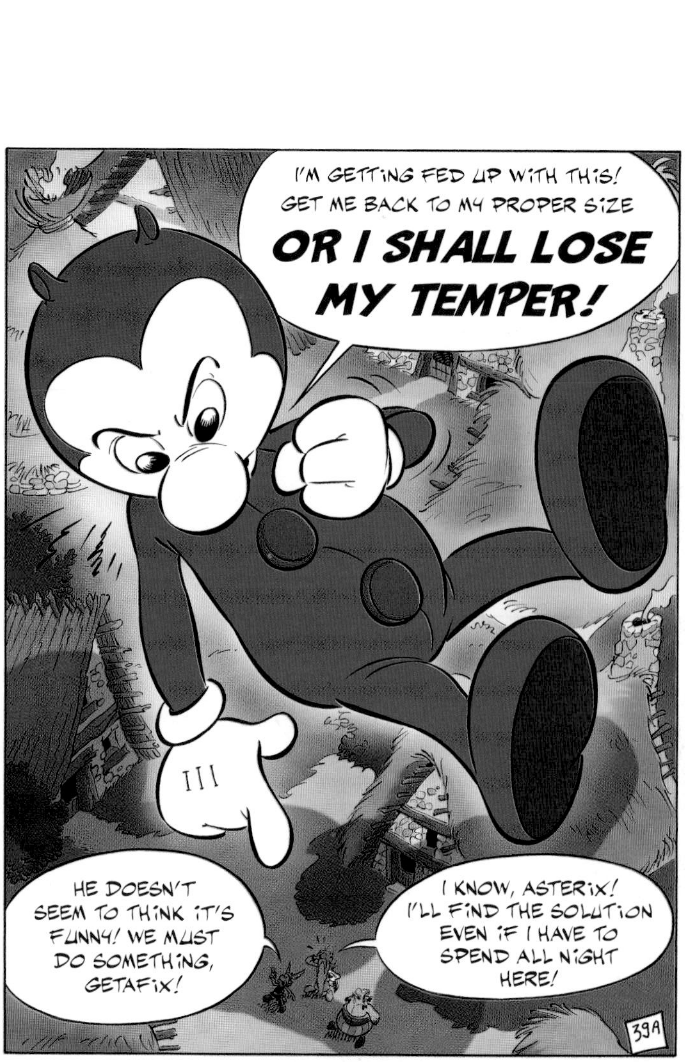
I'M GETTING FED UP WITH THIS! GET ME BACK TO MY PROPER SIZE OR I SHALL LOSE MY TEMPER!
HE DOESN'T SEEM TO THINK IT'S FUNNY! WE MUST DO SOMETHING, GETAFIX!
I KNOW, ASTERIX! I'LL FIND THE SOLUTION EVEN IF I HAVE TO SPEND ALL NIGHT HERE!

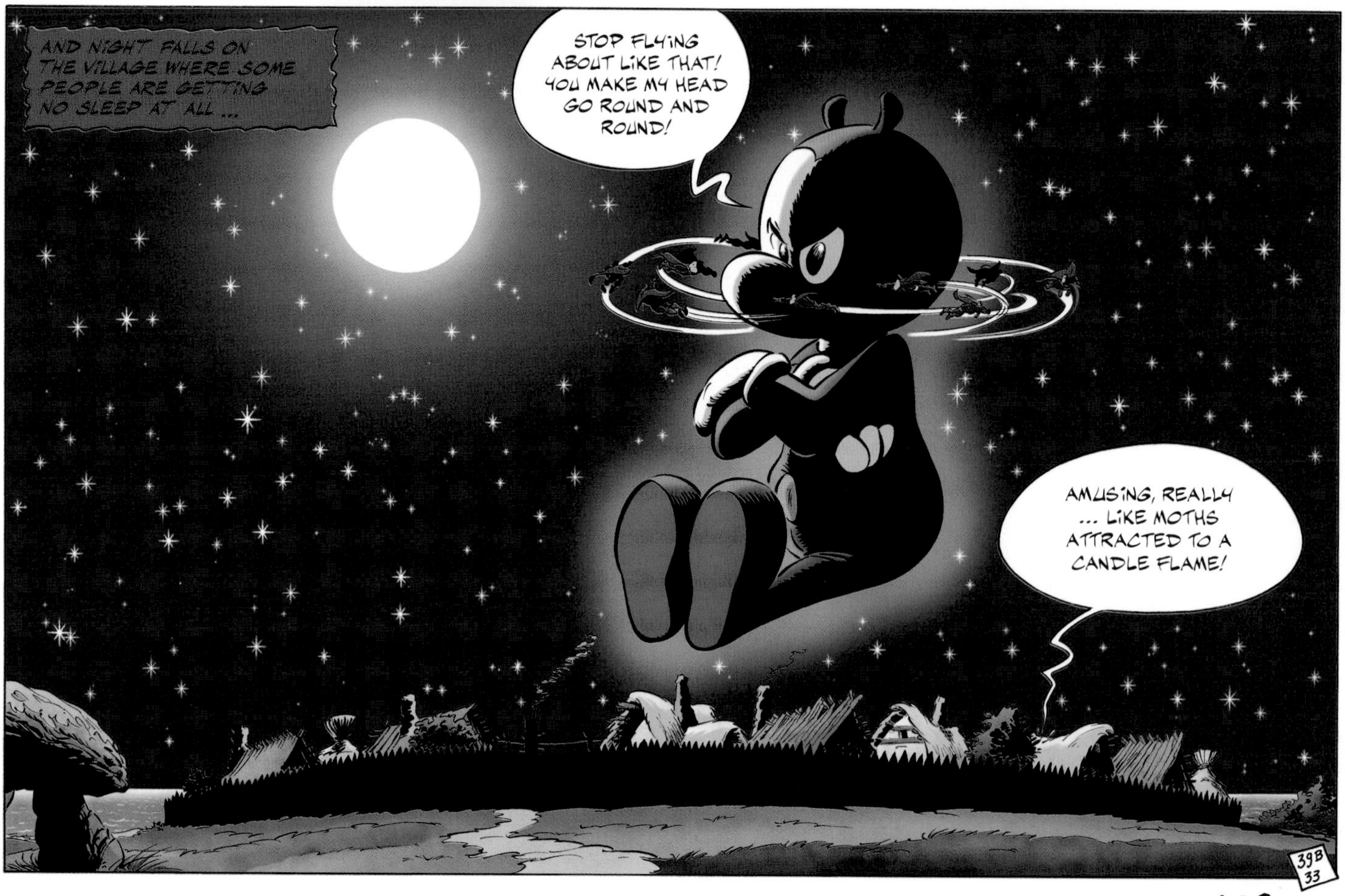
AND NIGHT FALLS ON THE VILLAGE WHERE SOME PEOPLE ARE GETTING NO SLEEP AT ALL ...
STOP FLYING ABOUT LIKE THAT! YOU MAKE MY HEAD GO ROUND AND ROUND!
AMUSING, REALLY ... LIKE MOTHS ATTRACTED TO A CANDLE FLAME!
UDERZO

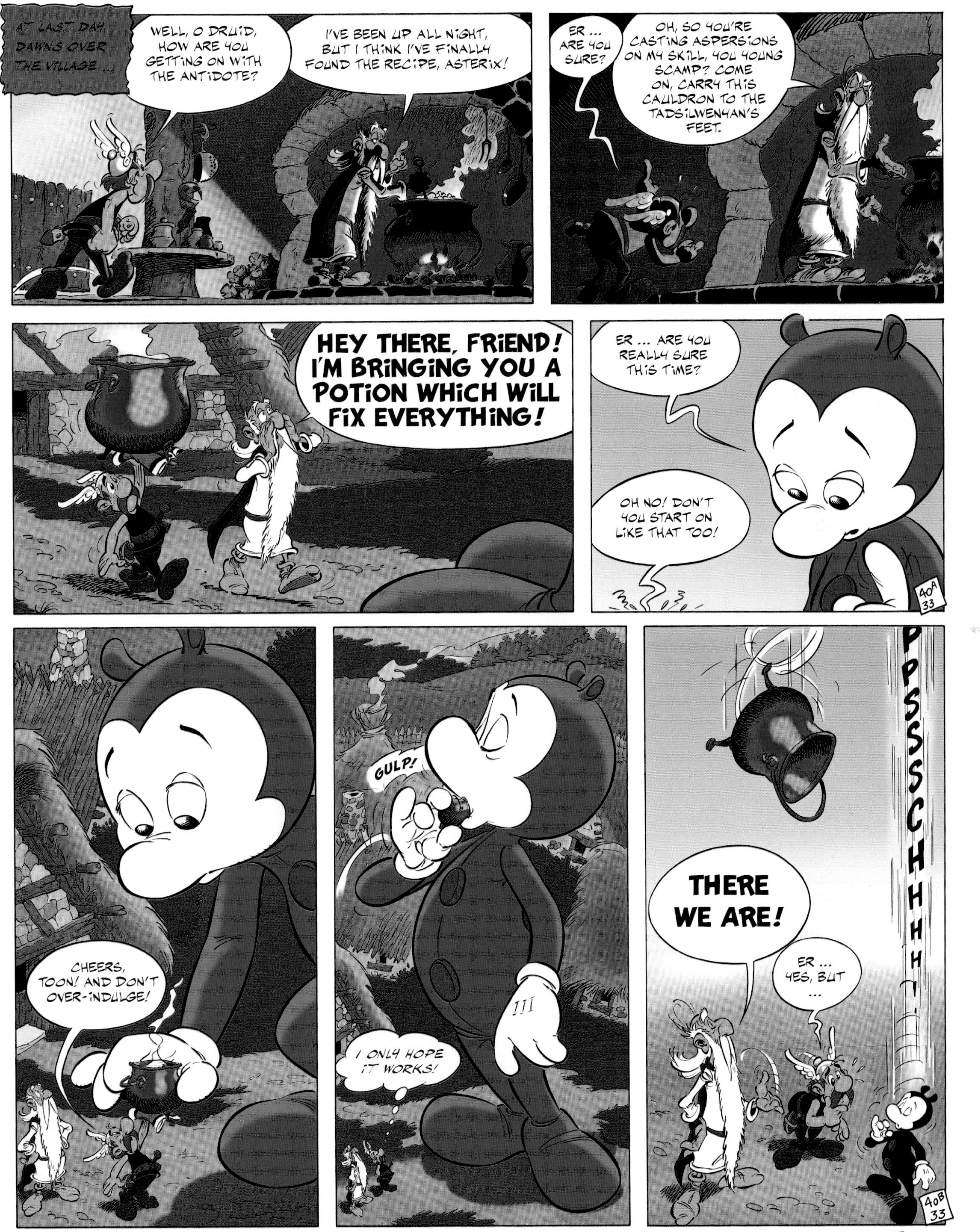

AT LAST DAY DAWNS OVER THE VILLAGE ...
WELL, O DRUID, HOW ARE YOU GETTING ON WITH THE ANTIDOTE?
I'VE BEEN UP ALL NIGHT, BUT I THINK I'VE FINALLY FOUND THE RECIPE, ASTERIX!
ER ... ARE YOU SURE?
OH, SO YOU'RE CASTING ASPERSIONS ON MY SKILL, YOU YOUNG SCAMP? COME ON, CARRY THIS CAULDRON TO THE TADSILWENYAN'S FEET.
HEY THERE, FRIEND! I'M BRINGING YOU A POTION WHICH WILL FIX EVERYTHING!
ER ... ARE YOU REALLY SURE THIS TIME?
OH NO! DON'T YOU START ON LIKE THAT TOO!
40A 33
CHEERS, TOON! AND DON'T OVER-INDULGE!
GULP!
I ONLY HOPE IT WORKS!
PPSSSCHHHHH!
THERE WE ARE!
ER ... YES, BUT ...
40B 33
UDERZO

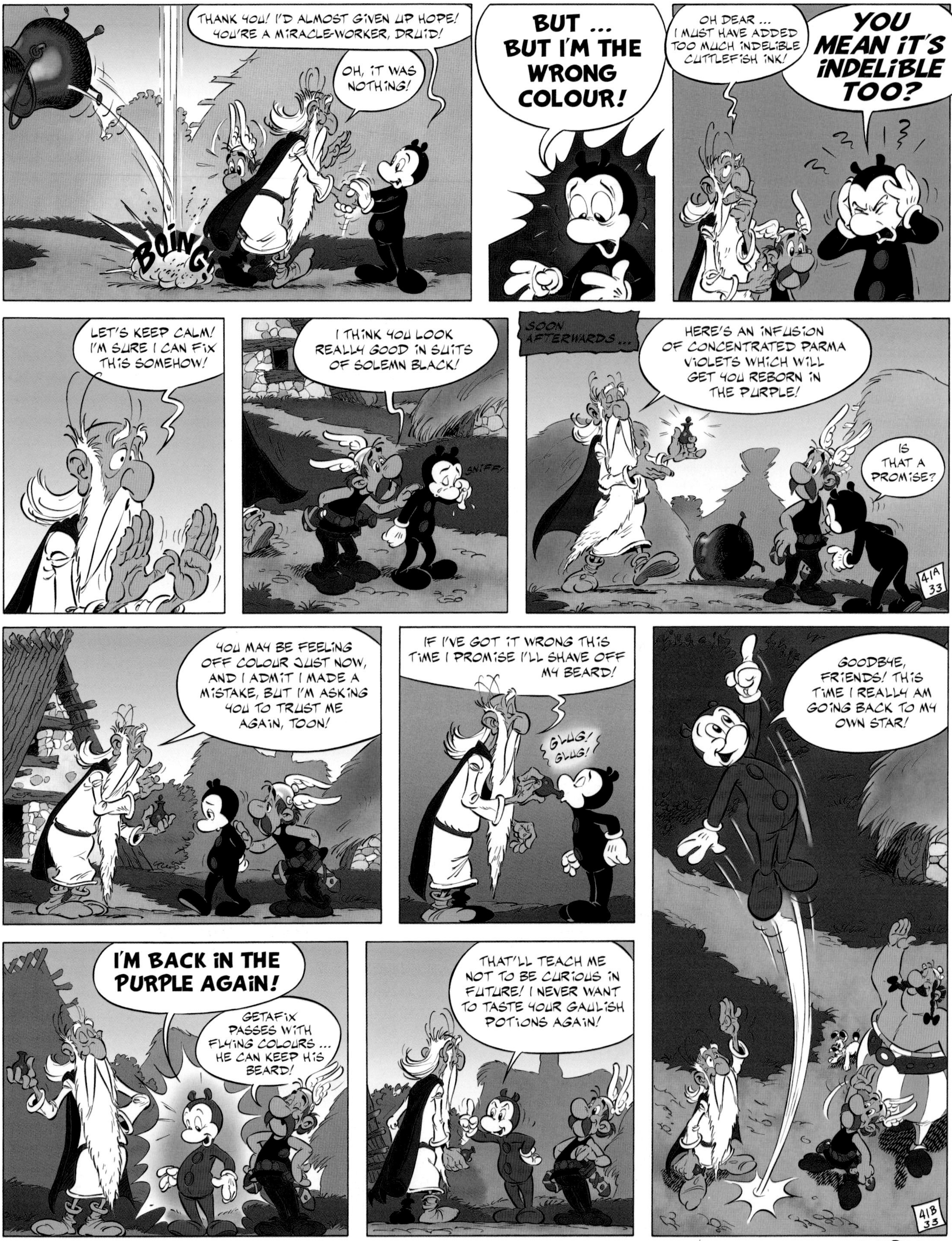
THANK YOU! I'D ALMOST GIVEN UP HOPE! YOU'RE A MIRACLE-WORKER, DRUID!
OH, IT WAS NOTHING!
BOING!
BUT ... BUT I'M THE WRONG COLOUR!
OH DEAR ... I MUST HAVE ADDED TOO MUCH INDELIBLE CUTTLEFISH INK!
YOU MEAN IT'S INDELIBLE TOO?
LET'S KEEP CALM! I'M SURE I CAN FIX THIS SOMEHOW!
I THINK YOU LOOK REALLY GOOD IN SUITS OF SOLEMN BLACK!
SNIFF!
SOON AFTERWARDS ...
HERE'S AN INFUSION OF CONCENTRATED PARMA VIOLETS WHICH WILL GET YOU REBORN IN THE PURPLE!
IS THAT A PROMISE?
YOU MAY BE FEELING OFF COLOUR JUST NOW, AND I ADMIT I MADE A MISTAKE, BUT I'M ASKING YOU TO TRUST ME AGAIN, TOON!
IF I'VE GOT IT WRONG THIS TIME I PROMISE I'LL SHAVE OFF MY BEARD!
GLUG! GLUG!
GOODBYE, FRIENDS! THIS TIME I REALLY AM GOING BACK TO MY OWN STAR!
I'M BACK IN THE PURPLE AGAIN!
GETAFIX PASSES WITH FLYING COLOURS ... HE CAN KEEP HIS BEARD!
THAT'LL TEACH ME NOT TO BE CURIOUS IN FUTURE! I NEVER WANT TO TASTE YOUR GAULISH POTIONS AGAIN!
UDERZO

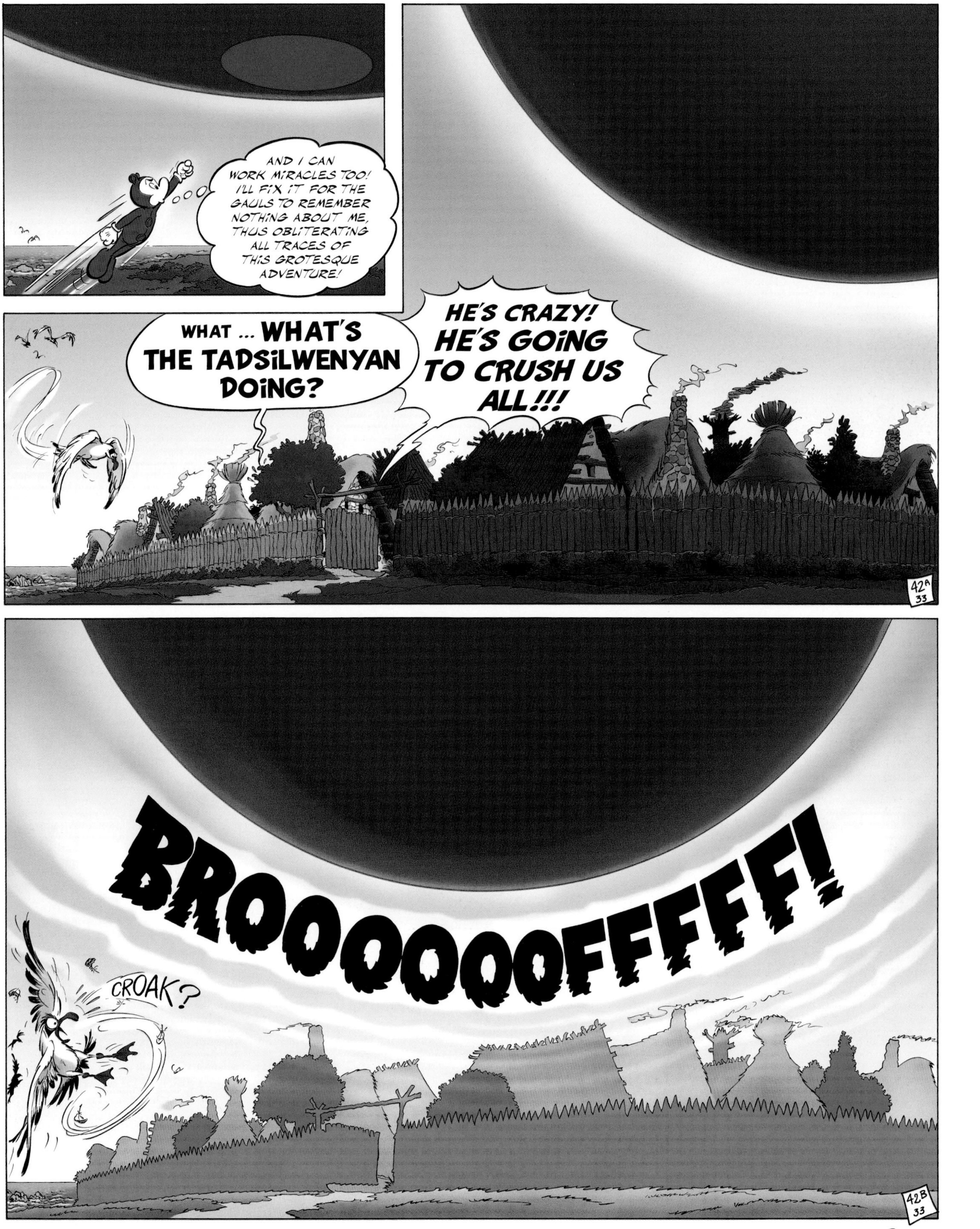
AND I CAN WORK MIRACLES TOO! I'LL FIX IT FOR THE GAULS TO REMEMBER NOTHING ABOUT ME, THUS OBLITERATING ALL TRACES OF THIS GROTESQUE ADVENTURE!
WHAT ... WHAT'S THE TADSILWENYAN DOING?
HE'S CRAZY! HE'S GOING TO CRUSH US ALL!!!
42A 33
BROOOOOOFFFFFF!
CROAK?
42B 33

-UDERZO-

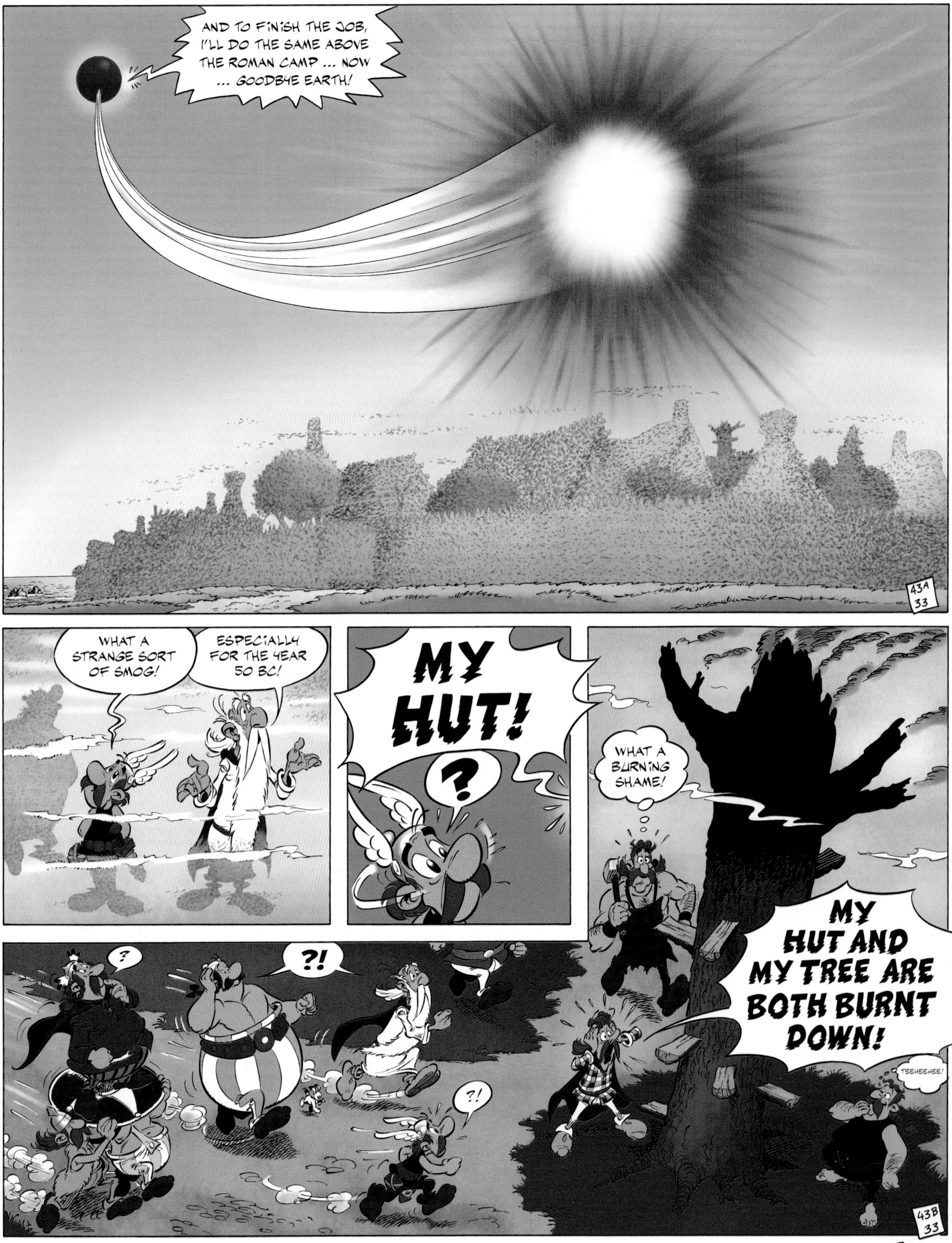
AND TO FINISH THE JOB, I'LL DO THE SAME ABOVE THE ROMAN CAMP ... NOW ... GOODBYE EARTH!
WHAT A STRANGE SORT OF SMOG!
ESPECIALLY FOR THE YEAR 50 BC!
MY HUT!
?
WHAT A BURNING SHAME!
MY HUT AND MY TREE ARE BOTH BURNT DOWN!
?
?!
?!
TEEHEEHEE!
UDERZO

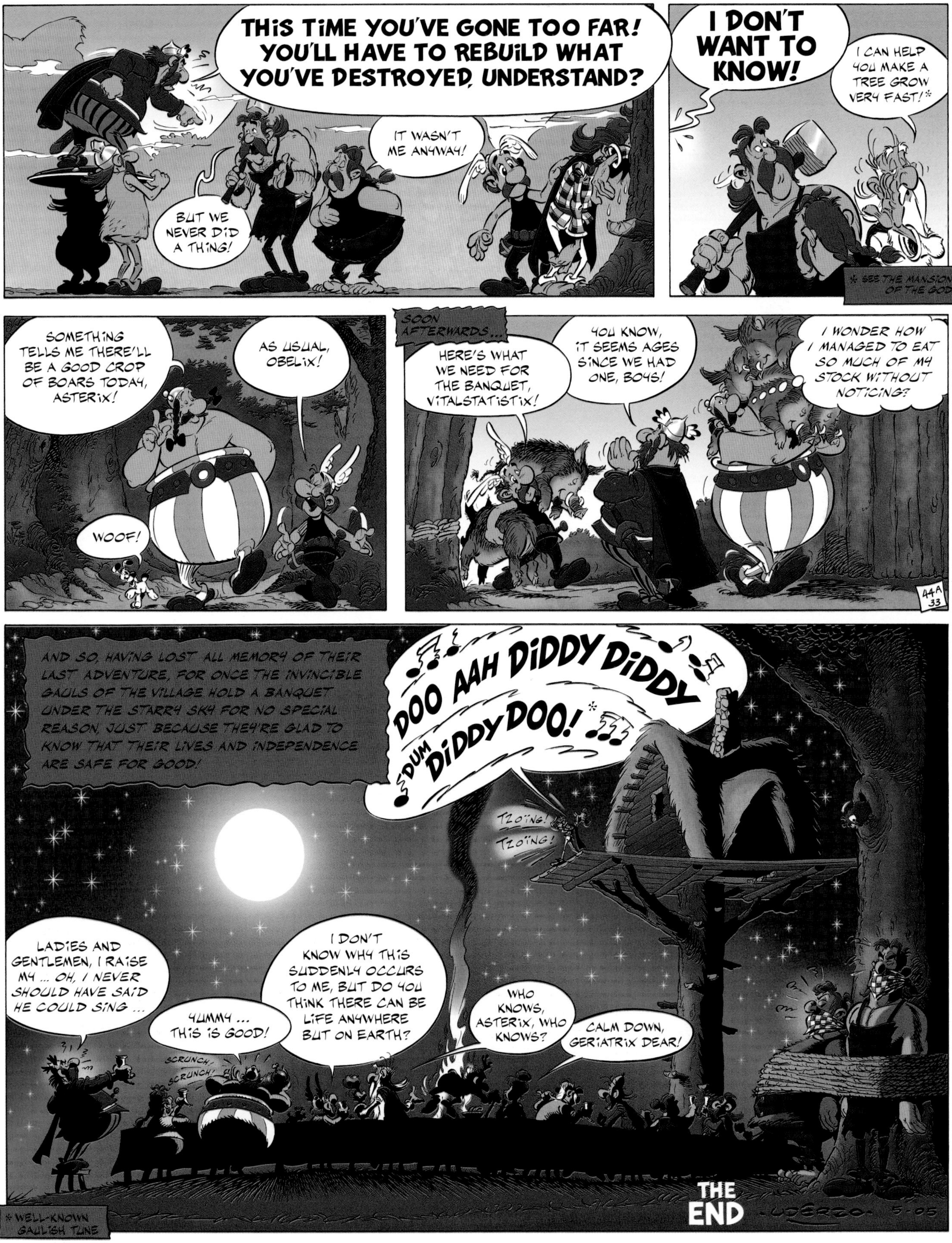
THIS TIME YOU'VE GONE TOO FAR! YOU'LL HAVE TO REBUILD WHAT YOU'VE DESTROYED, UNDERSTAND?
IT WASN'T ME ANYWAY!
BUT WE NEVER DID A THING!
I DON'T WANT TO KNOW!
I CAN HELP YOU MAKE A TREE GROW VERY FAST!*
* SEE THE MANSIONS OF THE GODS
SOMETHING TELLS ME THERE'LL BE A GOOD CROP OF BOARS TODAY, ASTERIX!
AS USUAL, OBELIX!
WOOF!
SOON AFTERWARDS...
HERE'S WHAT WE NEED FOR THE BANQUET, VITALSTATISTIX!
YOU KNOW, IT SEEMS AGES SINCE WE HAD ONE, BOYS!
I WONDER HOW I MANAGED TO EAT SO MUCH OF MY STOCK WITHOUT NOTICING?
44A 33
AND SO, HAVING LOST ALL MEMORY OF THEIR LAST ADVENTURE, FOR ONCE THE INVINCIBLE GAULS OF THE VILLAGE HOLD A BANQUET UNDER THE STARRY SKY FOR NO SPECIAL REASON, JUST BECAUSE THEY'RE GLAD TO KNOW THAT THEIR LIVES AND INDEPENDENCE ARE SAFE FOR GOOD!
DOO AAH DIDDY DIDDY DUM DIDDY DOO!*
TZOING! TZOING!
LADIES AND GENTLEMEN, I RAISE MY ... OH, I NEVER SHOULD HAVE SAID HE COULD SING ...
YUMMY ... THIS IS GOOD!
SCRUNCH! SCRUNCH!
I DON'T KNOW WHY THIS SUDDENLY OCCURS TO ME, BUT DO YOU THINK THERE CAN BE LIFE ANYWHERE BUT ON EARTH?
WHO KNOWS, ASTERIX, WHO KNOWS?
CALM DOWN, GERIATRIX DEAR!
THE END
UDERZO 5.05
* WELL-KNOWN GAULISH TUNE

'In this book I would like to pay tribute to the great creations of Tadsilweny... sorry, I mean the great creations of Walt Disney who, famous and amazing druid that he was, allowed some of his colleagues, myself included, to fall into the cauldron of a potion of which he alone knew the magical secret.'

Albert Uderzo

Asterix titles available now

1 Asterix the Gaul
2 Asterix and the Golden Sickle
3 Asterix and the Goths
4 Asterix the Gladiator
5 Asterix and the Banquet
6 Asterix and Cleopatra
7 Asterix and the Big Fight
8 Asterix in Britain
9 Asterix and the Normans
10 Asterix the Legionary
11 Asterix and the Chieftain's Shield
12 Asterix at the Olympic Games
13 Asterix and the Cauldron
14 Asterix in Spain
15 Asterix and the Roman Agent
16 Asterix in Switzerland
17 The Mansions of the Gods
18 Asterix and the Laurel Wreath
19 Asterix and the Soothsayer
20 Asterix in Corsica
21 Asterix and Caesar's Gift
22 Asterix and the Great Crossing
23 Obelix and Co.
24 Asterix in Belgium
25 Asterix and the Great Divide
26 Asterix and the Black Gold
27 Asterix and Son
28 Asterix and the Magic Carpet
29 Asterix and the Secret Weapon
30 Asterix and Obelix All at Sea
31 Asterix and the Actress
32 Asterix and the Class Act
Asterix and the Vikings
Asterix at the Olympic Games (film tie-in)
Asterix Omnibus (Books 1-3)
Asterix Omnibus (Books 31-33)

Coming soon

Asterix versus Caesar
The Twelve Tasks of Asterix
Asterix Conquers America
Operation Getafix
Asterix Omnibus (Books 4-6)
Asterix Omnibus (Books 28-30)

Original title: *Le Ciel Lui Tombe Sur La Tête*

Exclusive Licensee: Orion Publishing Group
Translators: Anthea Bell and Derek Hockridge
Typography: Bryony Newhouse
Inking: Frédéric Mébarki
Colour work: Thierry Mébarki
Co-ordination: Studio 56

This paperback edition first published in Great Britain in 2006 by Orion Books Ltd, Orion House, 5 Upper St Martin's Lane, London WC2H 9EA

5 7 9 10 8 6

Printed in Italy by Printer Trento S.r.l.

http://gb.asterix.com
www.orionbooks.co.uk

A CIP catalogue record for this book is available from the British Library

ISBN 978 0 75287 548 4

Distributed in the United States of America by Sterling Publishing Co. Inc., 387 Park Avenue South, New York, NY 10016

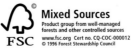

Mixed Sources
Product group from well-managed forests and other controlled sources
www.fsc.org Cert no. CQ-COC-000012
© 1996 Forest Stewardship Council